Acknowledgements

This treatment progra Dr. Joseph LaBrie and the Department of Student Affairs at Loyola Marymount University (LMU). Heads UP is a harm reduction-based drinking prevention and research project that seeks to promote healthy choices among all students. The program is indebted to each of the authors, as well as to all who have contributed to this ongoing research project over the years. We wish to thank Karie Huchting, Toby Lamb, Thomas Quinlan, Andrea Rodrigues, Alysha Thompson, Shannon Kenney, Jessica Cail, Ashley Sanford and the countless undergraduate research assistants who have passed through our doors. The persons who spent untold hours editing this manual and guiding it through the publication process are Savannah Migliuri and John Rohrbach. Their care and thoughtfulness have led to a manuscript that we hope will benefit the college alcohol risk reduction provider field. Our deepest thanks go to them.

There are many who have aided us in our mission to reduce risky student drinking and increase our understanding of the dynamics around student drinking. We would like to thank the Division of Student Affairs at Loyola Marymount University, especially Dr. Lane Bove, V.P. of Student Affairs; Dr. Linda McMurdock, Assistant V.P. of Student Affairs; as well as Fr. Robert Lawton, President of the University, Dean Michael Engh, S.J., and Dr. Cheryl Grills, Chair of the Department of Psychology, for their endless support. We are especially indebted to the Sponsored Projects Office, including Mark Bailey, Yolanda Uzzell, and Joseph McNicholas.

Special thanks to Dr. Mary Larimer, Dr. Clayton Neighbors, and Dr. Jason Kilmer for their training, support, and guidance. Thank you to Dr. Cheryl Grills for her consultation and direction.

The research of Heads UP would not have been possible without the generous support of several granting agencies, including the U.S. Department of Education, the National Institute of Alcohol Abuse and Alcoholism (NIAAA) of the National Institutes of Health, and the Alcoholic Beverage Medical Research Foundation (ABMRF). This manual was funded by the U.S. Department of Education, Office of Safe and Drug-Free Schools, Alcohol and Other Drug Prevention Models on College Campuses Grant.

Lastly, we would like to thank the thousands of college students who have participated in our research. The sharing of their experiences has not only aided our intervention efforts but also led us to better understand this issue from their perspective.

Contents

Introduction

Heads UP Overview

Heads UP is a multifaceted, harm reduction-based drinking prevention and intervention program designed for the college population. This manual is intended to help student affairs personnel and administration conduct primary and secondary interventions with those considered typically high risk, including first-year students as well as those sanctioned for alcohol-related offenses. Heads UP addresses the unique concerns of young people, particularly college students; this manual can be used as an aid to colleges and universities in implementing an effective and culture-changing alcohol program on campus. Furthermore, this manual is intended to help therapists and professionals working with people who have alcohol-related issues.

This manual provides specific steps regarding the implementation of an effective intervention program on a college campus, as demonstrated by Heads UP. Although the combination of assessment, intervention, and programming as outlined in this manual is ideal, pieces of the intervention process and overall program can also be effective in addressing the needs of your college, university, or organization. Because the Heads UP program is based on experimental evidence of effective interventions with college students, all components of the program are empirically sound.

A review of the etiology and epidemiology of college drinking is presented as a framework for understanding the importance of alcohol-related interventions. Each chapter provides an important backdrop against which to consider the intervention and to promote thoughtful and clear implementation of procedures, intervention, and programming. Specific techniques and procedures congruent with the theoretical underpinnings of Heads UP are provided. Specific resources may be found in the appendices.

Heads UP for High School

While the Heads UP protocol was originally designed for use on college and university campuses, it can be easily modified and adapted for use in high schools. If you are a high school administrator, you may consider using the Heads UP intervention program with classes, athletic teams, or advising groups. Due to the sex-specific nature of the program, it is best to conduct the intervention with single-sex groups and to tailor the intervention specifically to your students.

Chapter I

Alcohol Consumption and its Consequences for College Students

National Difficulties

If you're reading this manual, you're likely to have some idea of the impact of problematic alcohol use. However, research regarding the prevalence and epidemiology of problematic alcohol use is presented as a basis for understanding the widespread need for alcohol programs in the United States.

Alcohol use by college students is considered by some to be a mainstay of the college experience. Nationally, 80-90% of all underage college students drink (Haines & Spear, 1996), and 44% of college students report heavy episodic drinking (drinking five or more drinks for men and four or more for women, in one sitting). Twenty percent of students report such heavy episodic drinking three or more times during a two-week period (Wechsler, Lee, Kuo, & Lee, 2000).

The consequences of drinking for university communities are devastating. From missed classes to death and vandalism to sexual assaults, alcohol abuse leaves its mark. Nationwide, roughly 1,400 college students die each year from alcohol-involved accidental death (Hingson, Heeren, Winter, & Wechsler, 2005). In addition, approximately one-quarter of all students report that drinking has had a negative impact on their academic work through missed classes, poor test and assignment performance, and failure to keep up with coursework (Engs, Diebold, and Hanson, 1996; Wechsler, Davenport, Dowdall, Moeykens, & Castillo, 1994; Wechsler, Molnar, & Davenport, 1999). Drinking has also been associated with risky sexual behavior (LaBrie & Earleywine, 2000).

The psychological and interpersonal consequences of drinking affect most college students, both drinkers and non-drinkers, as well as the broader campus community. The National Institute on Alcohol Abuse and Alcoholism (NIAAA) Task Force, formed to study drinking on college campuses, reviewed the relevant research and concluded that "...the consequences of excessive drinking by college students are more significant, more destructive, and more costly..." than generally recognized (NIAAA Report, 2002). The report estimates 70,000 cases of sexual assault or date rape, 500,000 non-fatal injuries, 400,000 unprotected sex events, and 600,000 assaults of other students involve drinking annually. It has been estimated that nearly 5% of all college students have been involved with police or public safety officers due to drinking (Wechsler, Lee, Kuo, Seibring, Nelson, & Lee, 2002), 2.1 million students drive under the influence of alcohol each year (Hingson et al., 2005), and nearly 11% of students admit to vandalizing property after drinking (Wechsler et al., 2002).

Alcohol policy violations account for over 50% of all disciplinary actions on college campuses (Andersen & Gadaleto, 2001; Stone & Lucas, 1994). At schools with higher rates of heavy drinking, students also report a greater number of secondhand effects of alcohol use, including disruption of sleep or studies, property damage, and verbal, physical, or sexual violence (Wechsler, Moeykens, & Davenport, 1995). Therefore, alcohol use and abuse negatively affects the vast majority of college students in a variety of ways.

Specific Alcohol Use

Prior to your own implementation of Heads UP, we recommend compiling baseline data, including the demographic composition of the university or organization, as well as alcohol and drug norms, perceptions, and current programs. As an example, Loyola Marymount University's information is provided below. Examples of assessment, including specific measures and instruments, are given in Chapter VI.

If you are using the Heads UP program at a high school institution, it would be best to either conduct baseline data of student drinking at your institution and/or obtain national drinking statistics for high school students, ages 14-18. One resource is the Monitoring the Future Study (Bachman & Johnson, 1978; www.monitoringthefuture.org), an ongoing study of the behaviors, attitudes, and values of American secondary school students, college students, and young adults. It is important to gauge where your students are in relation to national averages, as well as to gain an understanding of the scope of problematic drinking and resulting problems at your particular institution.

In order to gain a better understanding of the efficacy of this program with our institution, a description of the student composition of LMU, scope of alcohol use at LMU, and efforts carried out at LMU to address alcohol-related consequences are provided. The Heads UP intervention has not yet been assessed in other settings.

Loyola Marymount University's Alcohol Use

Composition of LMU

Loyola Marymount University is a private, Catholic, mid-size university of approximately 5,500 full-time undergraduate students. The demographic composition of LMU for the fall semester of 2005 included students self-identified as African-American/Black (7%), Asian/Pacific Islander (13%), Hispanic (19%), Euro-American/White (57%), and declined to answer and other (4%). A strong majority of undergraduate students live on campus, including 97% of freshmen.

Scope of Alcohol Use at LMU

LMU experiences alcohol-related problems that compare to those at other colleges nationwide, such as alcohol poisonings, increased incidences of physical violence, and academic problems, to name a few. In order to get an overall picture of alcohol and drug use within the campus community, LMU participated in the CORE Alcohol and Drug Survey, the Cooperative Institutional Research Program CIRP survey, and the Electronic Check-Up To Go (E-CHUG), which included the World Health Organization's Alcohol Use Disorders Identification Test (AUDIT; Saunders, Aasland, Babor, De La Fuente, & Grant, 1993 – a measure of harmful alcohol use). The results revealed a disturbing pattern of problem drinking by LMU students. From the CORE data, 76.9% of all undergraduate students (71.4% of whom are under 21 years of age) reported drinking in the past 30 days, and 50% reported at least one episode of binge drinking in the same time period. Further, 2003-2004 AUDIT scores (as obtained through the E-CHUG) indicated that LMU students exceeded the cutoff score for alcohol problems. Therefore, LMU sought an effective intervention process to address the large amount of alcohol-related difficulties on campus.

Efforts to Address Alcohol-Related Problems at LMU

Over the past several years, LMU addressed the issue of drinking on campus in several concrete ways. Advertisements and posters promoting alcohol were banned from public spaces, including dorm windows. Student Housing has stringently enforced the university's policy of no underage drinking and no open containers. At present, all university-sponsored student events, many of which previously included alcohol consumption areas for students over 21, are alcohol-free. The CORE data reveals that students are beginning to get the message; 73.3% say that the campus is concerned about the prevention of alcohol and drug use. Yet, at the same time, 57.8% of students believe the social atmosphere on campus promotes drinking. Therefore, although drinking has been addressed in the past, it wasn't addressed sufficiently to reduce either problematic drinking or the perception of an alcohol-promoting culture on campus.

LMU's portrait of problem drinking and violations clearly revealed that freshmen (particularly freshman males) were at heightened risk for problems related to drinking. To reduce recidivism, Heads UP sought initially to target freshmen, particularly freshman males, to reduce alcohol-related problems, to build motivation to reduce drinking, and to effectively address alcohol-related violations with freshmen and others in the judicial system. The focus on freshman males was justified given the NIAAA Task Force report that first-year resident students may be at particular risk for alcohol misuse (NIAAA, 2002). Many students initiate a pattern of heavy drinking during their freshman year, increasing the likelihood that excessive drinking will interfere with successful adaptation to campus life and the fulfillment of an effective educational experience. Furthermore, Wechsler and his colleagues (1994) showed that patterns of binge drinking established during freshman year continue into later college years. Therefore, an intervention was needed to target freshman male students and those sanctioned for alcohol violations.

National Difficulties Specific to Women

Although the Heads UP program was originally designed for first-year males and judicially referred students, a unique intervention for women was subsequently developed. After a year of implementation of the men's program, it appeared that a female-specific program was needed. In 1999, the Harvard School of Public Health (HSPH) College Alcohol Study reported that national levels of binge drinking (drinking five or more drinks for men and four or more for women) and frequent binge drinking (bingeing three or more times in a two-week period) have remained fairly constant through the 1990s at about 44% for men and 23% for women (Wechsler et al., 2000). Examination of gender differences, however, reveals a different picture. While the statistics for men remained fairly steady, binge drinking among college women increased significantly (Wechsler et al., 2001).

According to studies from the Harvard School of Public Health (Wechsler et al., 2000, 2001), nearly 40% of college women binge drink regularly (defined as four or more drinks in a row at least once in the past two weeks). Women in sororities and on athletic teams appear to be at a greater risk, with 57% of team members and 80% of sorority residents identified as binge drinkers (Wechsler et al., 2000, 2001). In 1999, 42.6% of women reported binge drinking, up from 38.2% in 1993. Moreover, 24.8% of women in 1999 reported being drunk three or more times in one month—an increase from 18.9% in 1993 (Wechsler et al., 2000, 2001).

Another area of concern for women is frequent binge drinking, defined as bingeing three or more times during a two-week period. Forty-eight percent of college women say that a major reason for drinking is to get drunk. Those who engage in frequent binge drinking are seven to ten times more likely than non-binge drinkers to engage in unprotected and unplanned sexual activities, damage property, be injured, or get into trouble with campus police (Weschler, Davenport, Dowadall, Moeykens, & Castillo, 1994).

Similar to national trends, LMU experienced an increase in alcohol-related problems among its female population. Results from the CORE and CIRP surveys revealed a disturbing pattern of potentially problematic drinking by female students. In 2003, 57.6% of all incoming female freshmen reported drinking in the past 30 days, and 35% reported at least one episode of binge drinking in that time period.

The number of female LMU students whose behavior warranted citations by the police, public safety, or other campus authorities for alcohol-related offenses was rising. During the 2001-2002 academic year, women's alcohol-related offenses represented 14.4% of total judicial cases. In comparison, during the 2002-2003 academic year women's alcohol-related offenses had increased to 20.9% of the university's total judicial cases. For women only, during the 2001-2002 academic year, alcohol-related offenses accounted for 31.6% of their offenses, and in 2002-2003 it rose to 62.0% of all women's judicial offenses.

The national impact of alcohol on college women hit home at LMU in 2003 when several first-year female athletes were found unconscious due to their extreme alcohol consumption during a hazing incident. In response to this incident and the apparent increase in alcohol-related consequences across the female population at LMU, the Heads UP Women program was developed. Modeled after the original program, Heads UP Women aimed to target and intervene with first-year females to reduce alcohol-related problems, build motivation for reduced drinking, promote responsible drinking, and intervene effectively with females sanctioned by LMU's judicial affairs for alcohol offenses.

First-year females were targeted in the Heads UP Women program to reflect recent findings that women are particularly susceptible to a wide range of negative psychosocial and medical consequences. Additionally, an on-campus trend of women being sanctioned for alcohol offenses and treated for alcohol poisoning was noticed and addressed. As mentioned previously, the NIAAA Task Force report states that first-year resident students may be at particular risk for alcohol misuse (NIAAA, 2002). Many female students initiate a pattern of heavy drinking during their freshman year, increasing the incidence of alcohol poisoning and the likelihood that excessive drinking will interfere with successful adaptation to campus life and the fulfillment of an effective educational experience. In line with findings on men, Wechsler and his colleagues (1994) showed that patterns of binge drinking established as freshmen continue into later college years for women as well.

Chapter II

Heads UP Development

Why Not Traditional Treatments?

Current college alcohol prevention and treatment approaches can be classified into three major categories: (1) educational/awareness programs, (2) cognitive-behavioral skills-based programs, and (3) motivational/feedback-based approaches. Little evidence exists to support the use of education-based intervention programs (i.e., information/awareness, values clarification, etc.) for reducing alcohol use and/or alcohol-related negative consequences (Larimer & Cronce, 2002; Wechsler et al., 2002). While values-clarification and normative re-education both hold promise, they have yet to be evaluated using randomized trials (Larimer & Cronce). Multi-component skills-based approaches typically have educational components, but focus mainly on the acquisition of alcohol-related skills training (i.e., expectancy challenges, blood-alcohol discrimination training, and self-monitoring of alcohol use; Larimer & Cronce). Thus, neither educational/awareness programs nor cognitive-behavioral skills-based programs definitively address the consequences of college alcohol use and abuse. While educational/awareness programs have been ineffective in addressing alcohol-related problems on college campuses, other programs (e.g., cognitive-behavioral or multi-component skills-based) include educational components and have not yet been validated using randomized trials.

Why Heads UP?

Heads UP seeks to extend the work of the principal investigator on brief and effective motivational interventions with high-risk college students (LaBrie, 2002) by shifting emphasis to group interventions. Further, preliminary findings from a disciplinary program of the University of New Mexico provide support for a brief alcohol intervention, which incorporates educational, attitudinal, and skills-based components (Walters, Gruenewald, Miller, & Bennett 2001). Successful interventions, however, need to target both high-risk groups and the broader campus community (NIAAA Task Force Report, 2002). Heads UP employs a nested model of alcohol interventions, with the high-risk individuals, including first-year students and students involved in alcohol-related violations, at the center of the model. These high-risk students are nested in the broader student body, in the wider campus community, and in the whole institutional community of faculty, staff, parents, and university supporters. Thus, this project is multi-layered. The Heads UP Research Office—housed within Academic Affairs, specifically the Psychology Department—has been established to work closely with members of the campus community to study and reduce the negative impact of drinking on student and campus life.

As previously mentioned, educational programs have been largely ineffective in reducing problematic drinking, suggesting that problematic college drinking does not necessarily represent a lack of knowledge, but rather a lack of motivation to change. Therefore, targeted approaches that utilize motivational enhancement techniques might better assist students who drink heavily (Barnett, Tevyaw, & Fromme, 2004). Interventions designed to build motivation to change problematic behavior often follow the principles of Motivational Interviewing (MI; Miller and Rollnick, 2002). MI is a non-judgmental, non-confrontational, client-centered approach founded on the basic principles of expressing empathy, developing discrepancy, rolling with resistance, and supporting self-efficacy. MI strategies include helping students find inconsistencies between their goals and their current behavior, identifying intrinsic motivation to reduce problematic drinking, and helping students learn new strategies to deal with high-risk situations. Interventions that incorporate both traditional MI techniques and additional non-MI techniques or "interventions that have been specifically adapted for use by nonspecialists" (Rollnick et al., 1992) constitute Adaptations of Motivational Interviewing (AMIs). Several reviews affirm the efficacy of AMI interventions (Noonan & Moyers, 1997; Dunn, Deroo, & Rivara, 2001; Burke, Arkowitz, & Menchola, 2003), as well as the effective implementation of AMIs by clinicians not specializing in substance abuse treatment (Noonan & Moyers).

Heads UP intervenes with high-risk individuals through motivational enhancement groups as well as in the broader campus community through outreach efforts provided by Heads UP staff and through an institutional administrative collaboration involving LMU's Student and Academic Affairs. Heads UP also brings together significant stakeholders (faculty, staff, and student leaders) to provide normative data, discuss the role of alcohol on campus, promote awareness, and provide helpful hints for intervening in different sectors. The Heads UP Research Office serves as a principal contact regarding alcohol issues for student organizations (fraternities, sororities, service organizations, etc.), faculty, and staff, and disseminates information on the progress of campus prevention efforts.

Heads UP is a valuable program not only in its theoretical conception, but also in its efficacy with judicially sanctioned students and first-year students.

Heads UP Comprehensive Dual Program

Heads UP is a comprehensive program with two components, a men's-specific and women's-specific program. While the two programs work cohesively with the same aims, each has significant differences tailored to gender-specific issues. The original Heads UP program was designed for men, since much of the research shows that men are the higher risk drinkers, particularly freshman men (Engs & Hanson, 1985; Johnston, O'Malley, & Bachman, 2000; Rosenhow, 1998; Wechsler, Lee, Kuo, & Lee, 2000). However, a rise in heavy episodic drinking by women and resulting alcohol-related consequences appeared in the research (O'Malley & Johnston, 2002; Wechsler et al., 2002; Young, Morales, McCabe, Boyd, & D'Arcy, 2005). As previously discussed, an intervention specific to women was needed and thus created.

Although the Heads UP Women program was modeled after the original program designed for men, several modifications were made to address the specific needs of women. While women often drink for many of the same reasons as men, including reducing inhibitions, relaxing, and fitting in, Nancy Gleason points to a major difference between young men and women's reasons for drinking: young women's desire for intimate relationships (Vince-Whitman & Cretella, 1999). The strong perceived relationship between alcohol and intimacy places women at risk for many negative consequences that typically don't affect men. The NIAAA estimates that each year 70,000 cases of sexual assault or date rape and 400,000 unprotected sex events that involve drinking occur on American college campuses. Compared to men, women with drinking problems are at increased risk for depression, low self-esteem, alcohol-related physical problems, marital discord or divorce, spouses with alcohol problems, and drinking in response to life crises (McCaul & Furst, 1994).

Research continues to document greater alcohol consumption among men. Nevertheless, lower consumption among women does not necessarily equal less harm. In fact, there are inherent physiological gender differences in both the effects and metabolizing of alcohol (Perkins, 2000). Women have an elevated risk for health problems related to alcohol use even if they drink less than men. A major difference is the amount of alcohol needed to feel different levels of intoxication. Women become intoxicated more quickly than men at the same level of drinking (Jones & Jones, 1976). The average female carries more body fat, or adipose tissue, than the average male, and body fat contains little water. Consequently, most women have less body water to dilute the alcohol, leaving higher concentrations of alcohol in women's bodies. Thus, women obtain higher blood-alcohol concentrations (BAC) than men after drinking equal amounts of alcohol. In addition to absorption differences, women metabolize alcohol differently than men

(NIAAA, 1999). Women have less alcohol dehydrogenase—the enzyme that metabolizes alcohol—than men. Alcohol is first metabolized by gastric alcohol dehydrogenase in the stomach before entering systemic circulation. Frezza, DiPadova, Pozzato, Terpin, Baraona, and Lieber (1990) reported that early stomach metabolization of alcohol was decreased in women compared with men and was virtually nonexistent in alcoholic women. Thus, more alcohol enters the bloodstream as pure alcohol in women than in men. These differences in absorption and metabolism place women at greater risk for alcohol poisoning.

Due to the variance in the effects of alcohol between men and women, and the inherent psychosocial differences in communication and relation, Heads UP was created to be a sex-specific program, targeting the specific needs of women and men.

Chapter III

Theoretical Foundation

Stages of Change and Motivational Interviewing
In order to understand the underlying theoretical constructs behind the design of Heads UP, a brief summary of stages of change, MI theory, and MI techniques is provided. In addition, Adaptations of MI (AMIs) are discussed. Traditional MI style is done in a one-on-one setting; however, Heads UP utilizes a group AMI in order to reach the most students on campus. Prochaska and DiClemente (1984) developed the Transtheoretical Model of behavior change (TTM) based on their work examining the change process and individuals' readiness to change. The TTM disputed the idea that pre-treatment establishment of motivation was needed prior to facilitating behavior change. Rather, they viewed behavior change as dynamic, including the following stages: pre-contemplation, contemplation, preparation, action, and maintenance. The TTM set the stage for researchers to examine motivation as a variable that could be influenced. In addition, the TTM stressed that interventions could be structured differentially based on participants' stages of change. The TTM also addresses several processes of change in addition to the constructs of self-efficacy (Bandura, 1982) and decisional balance (Janis & Mann, 1977), suggesting that individuals weigh the pros and cons of behavior change prior to making a decision about behavior.

MI Theory and Techniques
Following the lead of Prochaska and DiClemente (1984), researchers identified individuals who were resistant to change or in the early stages of change, typically deemed hopeless cases in the past. MI was created to facilitate change based on each individual's position along the continuum of change. "Motivational Interviewing is a directive, client-centered counseling style for eliciting behavior change by helping clients to explore and resolve ambivalence" (Rollnick & Miller, 1995, p. 325). MI is founded on the basic principles of expressing empathy, developing discrepancy, rolling with resistance, and supporting efficacy.

MI was conceived as a reaction to typical helping relationships in several ways. For example, in typical helping relationships, advice can be experienced by a client as controlling. While resistance in a typical helping relationship is viewed as the client's issue, resistance in MI is attributed to a disconnect between the therapist and client, or the therapist and client not being in sync. Secondly, addressing or facing a problem often involves facing negative information about oneself. Thirdly, addressing problems can elicit many difficult affective states (e.g., anxiety, guilt, shame). All of the above mentioned situations tend to elicit a client's defenses, and thus behavior change becomes difficult (Miller & Rollnick, 2002).

From an MI perspective, individuals do not change because of ambivalence about changing. Individuals feel they are stuck or confused about committing to a change. Working through the ambivalence is essential in increasing motivation and thus facilitating change. MI attributes change to a discrepancy between an individual's behavior and goals, identified as importance; a feeling of self-efficacy, identified as confidence; and a commitment to the change process, identified as readiness. MI diffuses typical defenses of individuals by eliciting reasons for change from the client, thus creating an empowering sense of control (Miller & Rollnick, 2002).

"Change talk," or talk supporting motivation to change, can be elicited through open questions, or questions that evoke explanations rather than simple answers. Further, the types of change talk can be reinforced by affirmation, reflection, and summarizing the talk. Types of change talk include the identification of the following: problem recognition, a desire to change, reasons to change, a need to change, the advantages of change, the disadvantages of maintaining the status quo, an ability or feeling of confidence to change, and a commitment or intention to change (Miller & Rollnick, 2002).

MI theoretically is a developmentally sensitive approach in addressing change with college students as it promotes empowerment in making important life decisions, including the decision of how to drink, rather than requiring change in an authoritarian manner.

Adaptations to Motivational Interviewing (AMI)
Motivational Interviewing has typically been utilized on an individual basis between a therapist and a client. However, due to the demands of different populations (e.g., students) AMIs have been developed. Interventions that incorporate non-MI techniques with MI techniques or "interventions that have been specifically adapted for use by non-specialists" (Rollnick, Heather, & Bell, 1992) constitute adaptations of MI. Several reviews of AMIs have been conducted citing the effectiveness of AMI interventions (Noonan & Moyers, 1997; Dunn, Deroo, & Rivara, 2001, Burke, Arkowitz, & Menchola, 2003). Noonan and Moyers (1997) reviewed 11 studies regarding the use of brief MI interventions in the substance abuse domain and concluded that MI is generally effective with substance abusers. Dunn, Deroo, and Rivara (2001), noting the increased need for non-specialists to utilize opportunistic interventions, examined 29 studies of brief interventions adapted from MI. They found substantial evidence for MI as an "effective substance abuse

intervention method when used by clinicians who are non-specialists in substance abuse treatment" (Dunn et al., 2001, p. 1725).

Few studies have examined how to adapt the principles of MI for a group setting. One such study outlined a possible framework for using a four-session Group Motivational Intervention (GMI) to be used for patients with chemical dependency. The group sessions were structured with group leaders using a manual developed by the researchers. Therapists were trained to personalize the session for the individual patient while allowing the group to offer support and information (Foote et al., 1999). Each session employed different aspects of MI as well as other motivational techniques such as the use of "pros" and "cons" as a way to normalize feelings of ambivalence in patients. Sessions were being led through specific questions aimed at eliciting "change talk" and discussions about feelings of loneliness. In later sessions patients receive "tools of recovery" that can be used when the patient actively decides to change. Foote et al. (1999) admit that steps within the group must be taken in order to assure that ambivalence for each individual can be identified, that leaders can redirect "non-motivational" participation, and that the group acts as a positive reinforcement. The researchers believe that GMI as a structured intervention through the use of a group manual will help alleviate some of these concerns. Preliminary results suggest that the group sessions give a significantly greater sense of autonomy-supportiveness.

Lincourt, Kuettel, and Bombardier (2002) examined the utility of group adaptations to MI with clients mandated to substance abuse treatment who often prove highly resistant to interventions aimed at modifying behavior. Lincourt et al. (2002) assigned participants to receive a six-session group MI intervention prior to the standard treatment if they could not identify treatment goals upon intake. They found that group MI, when administered as an introduction to substance abuse counseling, increased the likelihood that participants would attend more treatment sessions. These findings are consistent with previous research (Brown & Miller, 1993) on group MI as a pretreatment intervention.

Therefore, in conjunction with the empirical support of other group AMIs (as cited above), the Heads UP program is a research-supported and effective AMI in alleviating alcohol problems on a college campus. Heads UP utilizes the principles of MI in order to promote individual changes within groups of students.

Chapter IV

Heads UP Goals and Initiatives

Goals of Heads UP
The Heads UP program seeks to reduce recidivism for alcohol-related judicial offenses, reduce the number of problems resulting from drinking for first-year students—particularly those who received the motivational enhancement intervention—reduce the negative costs/effects linked to alcohol, and positively enhance the campus culture as a whole through campus poster campaigns, faculty and staff involvement, and alcohol-related programming. In regard to women specifically, Heads UP seeks to:
- increase knowledge regarding the difference between responsible drinking and problem drinking among women,
- raise awareness of how problem drinking adversely affects women's health and puts female students at risk for alcohol poisoning, and
- lower the incidence of female students requiring medical care due to alcohol consumption, both in terms of EMT burden and transports to local hospitals.

Program Initiatives
Heads UP was created with: 1) initiatives targeting high-risk drinkers (first-year students and judicially referred students); 2) initiatives to change campus culture supported by the college administration; 3) initiatives directed by students; 4) initiatives that created a campus dialogue; 5) initiatives that provided infrastructure to the program's efforts; and 6) an evaluative initiative.

Intervention with High-Risk Drinkers Initiative
Initiatives for high-risk drinkers include the group motivational intervention with judicially referred alcohol offenders, which consists of a three-month follow-up of drinking habits and negative alcohol-related consequences. The same intervention is presented for general groups of incoming first-year students, who are recruited within their first month on campus. The first-year volunteer initiative also includes follow-up, but only for ten weeks, so that participants can complete the entire intervention by the end of their first semester on campus.

The centerpiece of this project is the motivational group intervention. This motivational-oriented intervention is specifically designed to address issues related to either male or female alcohol consumption. The intervention is research-based, involves trained personnel using motivational enhancement techniques, and includes a single ninety-minute to two-hour discussion group. The research-based motivational intervention is also tied to several linked and well-supported campus-wide initiatives.

The decision to develop sex-specific motivational interventions—a more intimate discussion format for women and a more lecture-type format for males—was based largely on the specific needs of female participants. Research findings indicate that focus group structure adds depth that may prove helpful in motivating behavior change (Greenbaum, 1993; Stewart and Shamdasni, 1990). The women's program organizes its group interventions into a focus group format to aid in understanding the context, influences, and motivations accompanying drinking among undergraduate females, and to allow for active participation by the participants.

Judicial Component

Throughout each semester, students receiving judicial violations involving drinking are sanctioned to attend the Heads UP group intervention. Once enrolled, these students participate in a brief, sex-specific focus-group intervention. At LMU, it is anticipated that each year 200 to 300 students will participate in Heads UP as part of a judicial sanction. The program is non-confrontational, allowing students to both assess their drinking and build motivation for changing their drinking. The facilitators are trained personnel, but are not judicial officers. They emphasize to the students that all data collected as part of the program is confidential and is in no way shared with Judicial Affairs or associated with any future sanctions. Facilitators inform Judicial Affairs only whether or not the student completes each aspect of the program. Failure to comply may result in further sanctioning (e.g., fines, academic probation). If a student chooses to not come through Heads UP, he or she is given an alternative sanction by Judicial Affairs. However, most students choose to attend Heads UP due to its non-confrontational and empathic style.

First-Year Volunteer Component

At the beginning of the fall semester of each academic year, 200 to 300 first-year male and 200 to 300 first-year female students are randomly selected and invited to participate in the Heads UP program. These students are recruited with letters sent to their home address and to their campus mailbox, as well as an email to their new university email address, highlighting the goals and protocol of the program as well as the incentives for participation. Participants receive monetary compensation for their participation. Approximately half of the women who participate are randomly assigned to participate in a control condition, in which they attend a forty-five-minute session and complete a Timeline Followback (TLFB), as well as complete a ten-week drinking follow-up. Once enrolled, these students participate in the same brief motivational enhancement group as the judicial offenders. These participants sign consent forms and are informed that all information they provide is confidential. The goal is that those underclass students who participate in the intervention will reduce judicial sanctions for alcohol-related incidents, as well as reduce problems related to drinking (including incidence of alcohol poisonings), as compared to peers not receiving the intervention.

Administrative Initiative

Leadership from top administrators, especially university presidents, is crucial to the successful implementation of plans to prevent problem drinking, as well as setting the tone for the campus culture with respect to alcohol use (DeJong, 1998; Mara, 2000). The NIAAA Task Force report (2002) cites evidence that experiences during the first six weeks of school for freshmen affect subsequent success in college. The report suggests alerting both parents and students to the possibility that heavy drinking derails a successful adaptation to college life and that a notification to parents and students may help prevent development of problems during this critical period. Heads UP gives parents and new freshmen a "Heads UP" on this possibility.

Rev. Robert Lawton, S. J., president of Loyola Marymount University, who is an enthusiastic supporter of Heads UP, sends out two letters annually, one month before the academic year begins. One letter addresses students directly, welcoming them to the university, advising them of the critical period of their first weeks on campus, describing some of the negative consequences of problem drinking, and encouraging them to develop healthy patterns and to discuss these issues with their parents. The second letter addresses first-year parents and encourages them to talk to their first-year son or daughter about alcohol before school begins and to stay actively involved in their lives throughout college. This presidential initiative aims to set the institutional tone regarding drinking while raising awareness for first-year students and their parents of how problem drinking can negatively affect their college success.

Student-Directed Initiative

Each year, Heads UP personnel and outside contractors conduct MI training for Resident Advisers (RAs) and Resident Directors (RDs), using role-play techniques for common situations that arise with students. RDs and RAs then lead normative feedback sessions in the first-year residence halls. At these mandatory meetings, freshmen receive administrative summaries of the university's CORE survey data and the RDs lead a discussion of significant points as well as provide campus norm information. Students, particularly the heaviest drinkers, often overestimate the amount of drinking done by their peers in order to justify their drinking level (Baer et al., 2001). There is significant evidence that correcting misperceptions about campus drinking and false beliefs about the number of students who drink excessively has been successful in short-term attitude and drinking changes (Clapp & McDonnell, 2000; DeJong & Linkenbach, 1999; Perkins, 2002; Perkins & Wechsler, 1996). This discussion seeks to correct misperceived norms, especially among problem drinkers.

Campus Culture Initiatives
Campus Poster Campaign
Heads UP has developed a social norms media campaign that seeks to increase awareness about student health issues surrounding alcohol use and increase general student awareness of their personal drinking behaviors in relation to their peers at LMU. Our hope is that this will, at the very least, encourage students to drink responsibly and stay within their limits.
This campaign is assisted by the Graphic Arts Department at LMU. Graphic arts students aid Heads UP in the design of a poster campaign as part of either a class or senior project. The posters are specific to LMU and contain facts about alcohol use on campus (particularly noting gender-specific statistics), as well as the effects of alcohol on the human body, with special attention to alcohol poisonings.

It is believed that campus-specific graphics and facts/information will make the message more "sticky" (Gladwell, 2000) and salient to students. The campaign involves several different posters placed throughout campus at regular time intervals. The goal of the campaign is to impact the campus with respect to student alcohol use patterns, community perceptions about local alcohol use, and policy and procedures that support safe drinking practices. DeJong et al. (1998) has termed this public health approach "environmental management" and emphasizes the responsibility that institutions of higher education have in creating prevention policies that establish and maintain a healthy and safe environment for all students.

Campus Programming Initiative
As part of its aims, Heads UP has taken on the responsibility for increasing awareness of campus alcohol policy and disseminating information based on program evaluation. In addition, Heads UP staff coordinates with other campus departments within Student Affairs and Academic Affairs (e.g., Residence Life, Student Psychological Services, student government, fraternities/sororities, Student Health Services, Campus Recreation, Ethnic and Intercultural Services, Public Safety, and EMTs) to hold specific anti-problematic drinking programs. Heads UP sponsors National Collegiate

Alcohol Awareness Week each year by hosting and co-hosting alcohol awareness events on campus. Some events may include an alcohol awareness fair, a mock party, and convocation hour events in which Heads UP personnel present salient social norms information in fun and interactive ways. With each set of posters released for the poster campaign, Heads UP hosts an event open to all students to release the student-designed posters and increase awareness of the initiative on campus. The goal of both the poster campaign and the programming initiative is to change campus culture by increasing mindfulness of personal and peer drinking behaviors and the negative alcohol-related consequences associated with that behavior.

In addition, Heads UP was founded as a responsible-drinking program, not an abstinence-based program; therefore, part of changing campus culture is meeting students "where they are at" and creating a comfortable and safe environment for students to express their thoughts and opinions on the drinking culture at their university.

Campus Dialogue Initiative
Heads UP initiated a series of campus lunch discussions, open to students, faculty, and staff, on the issue of student drinking and its impact on campus. At these lunches, normative feedback was given, participants discussed their views on drinking and the university's response to problem drinking, and participants learned how to use MI to intervene with people at risk. The goal of these lunches was to communicate the seriousness of the university's response to alcohol and to receive feedback from stakeholders on how the university's response might be improved. Another goal was to increase faculty involvement in campus alcohol issues. The faculty was given advice on how to include issues related to alcohol misuse in their courses.

Evaluation Initiative
The success of the group interventions is measured objectively. (Results can be found in the efficacy section of this manual). The success of all initiatives in changing campus attitudes and subjective norms regarding drinking across campus groups is evaluated via objective and process measures.

Creating Goals and Initiatives That Work at Your Institution
In order to develop an effective intervention, an assessment of current problematic alcohol use is essential (examples of assessment can be found in Chapter VI). Following a thorough assessment, goals and initiatives help shape the intervention, programming, and outcomes expected in each identified, problematic area. The aforementioned goals and initiatives can be modified to accommodate the needs of your school, university, or organization.

Chapter V

Efficacy of Heads UP

Efficacy of Heads UP Men
The PI conducted a preliminary motivational intervention study with college males at risk for problems associated with drinking and risky sex (LaBrie, 2002). The study examined how a decisional balance protocol (i.e. weighing the pros and cons of a specific behavior) affected alcohol consumption and risky sexual behavior, as well as modified motivational intervention and intentional variables. The study incorporated several principles from MI. Ninety-three male college students who reported drinking more than twice per week and who had two or more sexual partners in the previous two months participated in the study. These subjects were randomly assigned to one of two groups: 1) a safer-sex group or 2) an alcohol reduction group. Each group received a decisional balance, the first for increased condom use, and the second for reducing drinking. Thus, each group served as a control for the other. In the alcohol decisional balance group, each participant was asked to list his personal reasons for drinking less than he did at present and his reasons against drinking less. After listing his reasons for and against change, the participant responded to a series of open-ended, non-directive questions about why the reasons he listed for change were important to him. The decisional balance followed an extensive calendar review of each participant's sexual and drinking behavior over the past three months. Thus, participants were primed to think about their behavior.

For the alcohol group, this brief motivational intervention proved effective in increasing motivation to drink less, decreasing intended drinking over the next month, and, most significantly, reducing drinking over a thirty-day follow-up period (LaBrie, Pedersen, Earleywine, & Olsen 2005). These results suggest, along with the other research (NIAAA 2002), that brief motivational interventions may be effective in changing drinking intentions and behavior. This preliminary data used an individual intervention. We sought to extend this intervention, enhanced with other motivational enhancement techniques, to groups of high-risk individuals.

The NIAAA Task Force (2002) notes that strong evidence supports the effectiveness of interventions that (1) simultaneously address alcohol-related attitudes and behaviors, (2) use survey data to counter students' misconceptions about their fellow students' attitudes toward excessive drinking and drinking practices, and (3) increase students' motivation to change their drinking habits. Programs that combine these three empirically validated approaches have proven the most effective in reducing problem drinking (Larimer & Cronce, 2002). Heads UP Men did just this. The program sought to build upon the previously mentioned preliminary study while incorporating norms clarification and cognitive behavioral skills with motivational enhancement techniques to address both attitudes and behaviors. The Heads UP Men program has proved advantageous both for freshman males as well as those sanctioned by judicial affairs as a result of alcohol violations.

Efficacy of Intervention with Freshman Males
The effect of the freshman Heads UP Men groups (intervention) has been positive, as measured by changes in drinking across time (from pre-intervention to third month post-intervention). Since the inception of Heads UP, there have been several changes in student drinking patterns and related problems. Over the course of two years, 239 freshman male students participated in the intervention. During Year 1 of the project, 120 freshman males volunteered for the intervention with a three-month follow-up (75% completed); during Year 2 of the project, 119 freshman males volunteered for the intervention with a three-month follow-up (77% completed). Of the 239 freshman volunteers, 195 drank alcohol. At the three-month follow-up, these 195 students significantly reduced their mean reported total drinks per month by 39%, from 53.16 to 32.31 drinks ($p < .001$), drinking days per month by 32%, from 7.24 to 4.95 days per month ($p < .01$), and maximum drinks consumed at one time by 34%, from 10.73 to 7.11 drinks ($p < .01$) (see Figure 1). (Please note that all figures are copyrighted.)

Figure 1-I

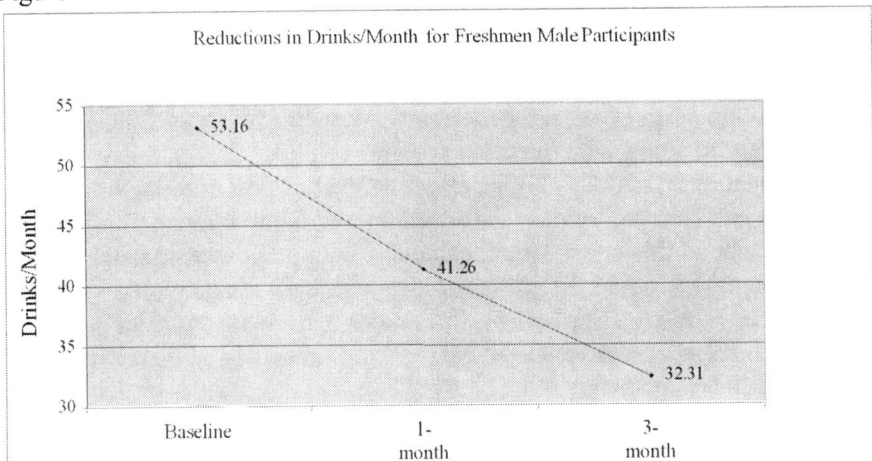

Reductions in Drinks/Month for Freshmen Male Participants

© LaBrie, Lamb, Pedersen, & Quinlan, 2006.

Figure 1-II

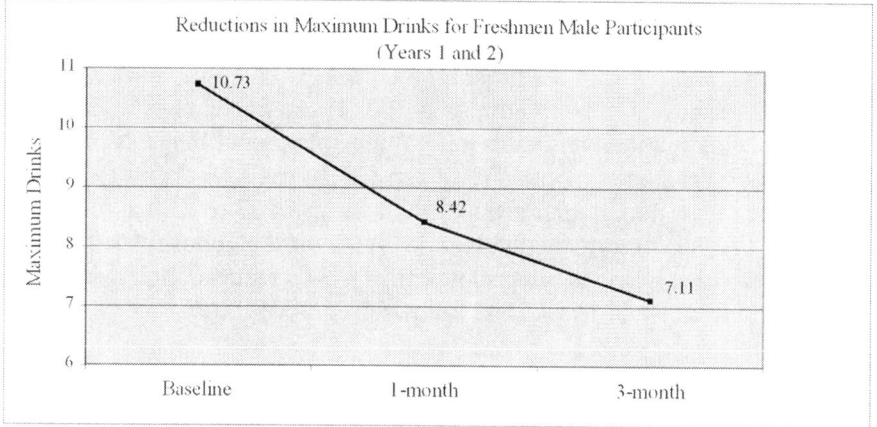

Reductions in Maximum Drinks for Freshmen Male Participants (Years 1 and 2)

© LaBrie, Lamb, Pedersen, & Quinlan, 2006.

To provide evidence for the preventative effects of the intervention, drinker type in the last two weeks (Wechsler & Nelson, 2001) from the pre-intervention Timeline Followback (TLFB) was compared with drinker type in the last two weeks of the participants' third-month diary. Based on drinking habits in the last two weeks of the TLFB, participants were either classified as non-drinkers (no drinking in the past three months of diaries), non-binge drinkers (drank four or less drinks on drinking occasions in the last two weeks of the third month diary), binge drinkers (drank five or more drinks in a row once or twice in the last two weeks of the third-month diary), and frequent binge drinkers (drank five or more drinks in a row three or more times in the last two weeks of the third-month diary).

For the freshman male volunteers, 44% stayed the same drinker type from pre-intervention to three-month follow-up, and 36% decreased their drinker type to a lower drinking label from pre-intervention to three-month follow-up. Examined more closely, 93% of the non-drinkers who finished three months of follow-up continued to not drink at three-month follow-up, and 65% of non-binge drinkers stayed non-binge drinkers or became non-drinkers at three-month follow-up. Forty percent of binge drinkers became non-drinkers or non-binge drinkers at follow-up, and 31% of frequent binge drinkers became non-drinkers or non-binge drinkers at follow-up. Only 20% of participants increased drinker type to a higher drinking label.

The following analyses highlight the findings found separately in Year 1 and Year 2 of the project. All results include students who drank at least once in the three months before the intervention.

Year 1: Freshman Volunteers (n = 120)
Freshman volunteers reduced their drinks per month by 51%, from 47.23 to 23.18 drinks, and reduced their maximum drinks at one time by 46%, from 9.85 to 5.35 drinks at three months ($p < .05$). Those freshmen who drank the most preceding the intervention benefited most. Frequent binge drinkers reduced their drinks per month 57%, from 121.14 to 51.60 drinks ($p < .05$) and reduced their maximum drinks by 46%, from 16.73 to 9.00 at follow-up ($p < .01$). Finally, freshman volunteers with the most alcohol-related problems (≥ 7 problems in the past month, $n = 34$), reduced their drinks per month 52% from 94.57 to 44.95 at follow-up ($p < .05$).

A cohort of freshmen who did not participate in a Heads UP group ($n = 49$), but had similar demographics to the Heads UP group, was recruited during the third follow-up month to compare the same month drinking behavior of non-intervention with the intervention students. Non-intervention freshmen were found to drink significantly more than intervention freshmen in quantity of drinks per month (71% more, 81.42 vs. 23.18 drinks, $p < .001$), and other drinking variables assessed (all $p < .001$, Figure 2-I).

We compared alcohol-related sanctions received by the 120 Heads UP freshmen versus all other freshman males ($n = 374$). As compared to the Heads UP freshman participants, freshmen not participating in Heads UP were twice as likely to receive one sanction (47% vs. 23%, $p < .01$) and 3.33 times as likely to receive multiple sanctions (10% vs. 3%, $p < .05$) (Figure 2-II). Heads UP appeared successful at meeting program goals to reduce both heavy drinking and citations among freshmen.

Figure 2-I

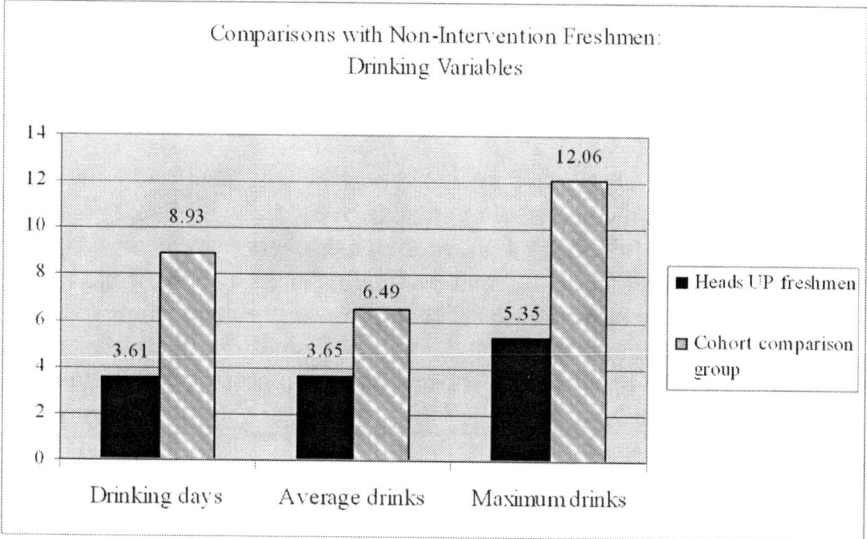

Comparisons with Non-Intervention Freshmen: Drinking Variables

© LaBrie, Pedersen, Lamb, & Quinlan, 2007.

Figure 2-II

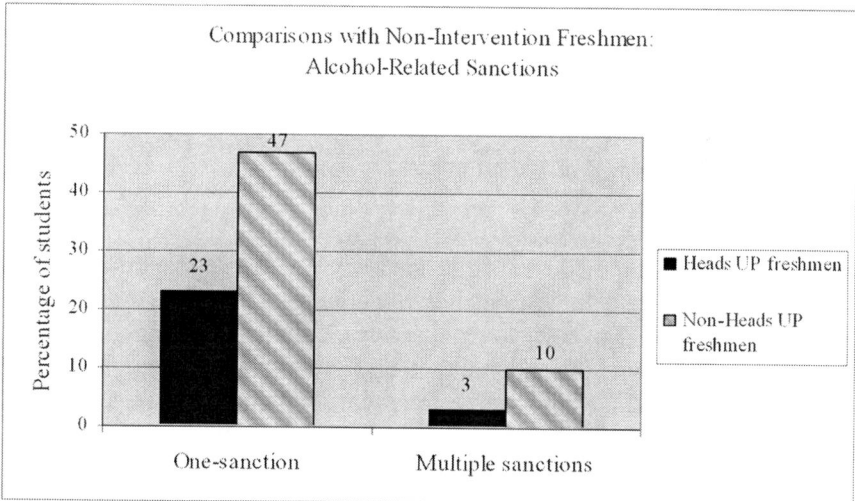

Comparisons with Non-Intervention Freshmen: Alcohol-Related Sanctions

© LaBrie, Pedersen, Lamb, & Quinlan, 2007.

Year 2: Freshmen Volunteers (n = 119)

During Year 2 of the project, the 119 freshman volunteers significantly reduced reported drinks per month by 26%, from 50 to 37 drinks at three-month follow-up ($p < .05$). At the three-month follow-up, freshman volunteers reduced drinking days by 1.65 ($p < .05$), average drinks by 1.00 drink ($p < .05$), and maximum drinks consumed during one occasion by 2.56 drinks ($p < .01$). All freshman volunteers also showed a reduction in their alcohol-related problems by approximately 52% at the three-month follow-up ($p < .01$).

During Year 2, the intervention again showed the best results with the heaviest drinkers and those who reported the most alcohol-related problems. At the three-month follow-up, frequent binge drinkers reduced drinks per month by 26.43 drinks ($p < .05$) and maximum drinks by 3.00 drinks ($p < .05$). Those with the most reported alcohol-related problems (more than six problems in the past month) reduced drinks per month by 38.00 drinks at three-month follow-up ($p < .05$). Those with the highest alcohol-related problems at pre-intervention also reduced problems by 40% at the one-month follow-up ($p < .001$) and by 67% at the three-month follow-up ($p < .001$).

Drinking variables from non-intervention freshman males were collected from the 2005 CORE survey. The month of the CORE survey was similar to the third month of data collected from the intervention freshmen. Compared with intervention freshman drinkers, non-intervention freshman drinkers ($n = 76$) drank more drinks per occasion (5.74 vs. 4.82, NS), more maximum drinks at one time (9.36 vs. 7.65, NS), had more binge drinking occasions in the past two weeks (2.41 vs. 1.54, $p < .01$), and had 86% more alcohol-related problems in the past month ($p < .01$). Figure 3-I below displays differences in drinking variables for intervention and non-intervention freshmen during Year 2 of the project.

Judicial records for the 2004-2005 academic year revealed that the 119 freshman volunteers who participated in the intervention were almost one and one-half times less likely to receive one alcohol-related sanction after the intervention than those 367 freshman males who did not receive the intervention ($p < .05$). Additionally, intervention participants were less likely to receive multiple sanctions than non-intervention freshmen (NS) (see Figure 3-II).

Figure 3-I

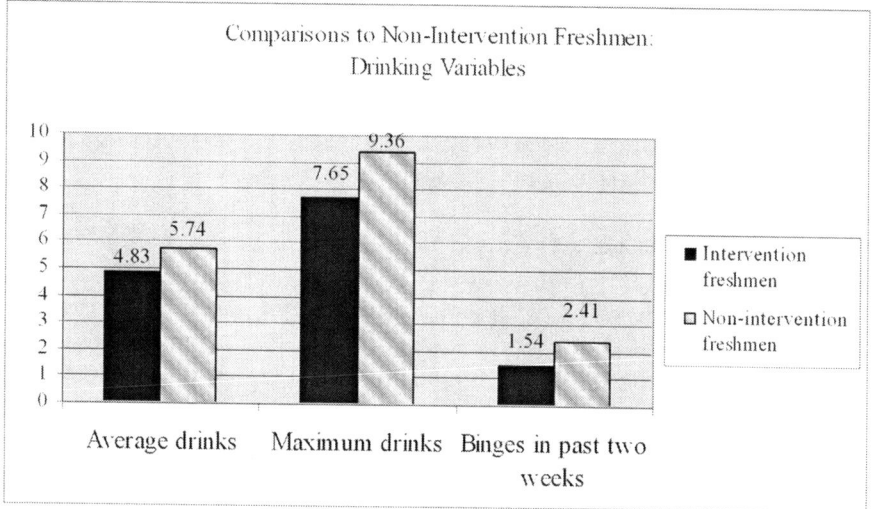

Comparisons to Non-Intervention Freshmen: Drinking Variables

Figure 3-II

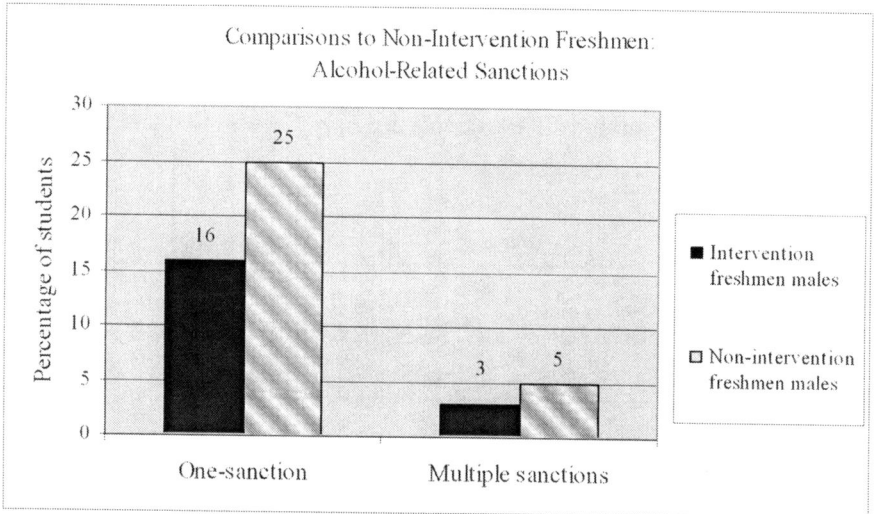

Comparisons to Non-Intervention Freshmen: Alcohol-Related Sanctions

© LaBrie, Lamb, Pedersen, & Quinlan, 2006

The Heads UP Men project was successful in intervening with freshman male students. In addition, the Heads UP Men program had great initial impact in bringing the issue of problem drinking to the forefront of university dialogue. It roused campus groups and has created a structured network of alcohol prevention efforts among previously unconnected parts of the campus community (i.e., neighbor relations, Academic Affairs, and Student

Affairs). The freshman males responded very favorably to the group intervention. Based on feedback reported by the participants, they found the groups engaging and helpful and left feeling empowered to make choices for themselves. Furthermore, Heads UP Men's success and the response of the students have deepened the commitment of university administrators to deal with problem drinking. (Please note that Figures 1, 2, and 3 are originally cited in LaBrie, Pedersen, Lamb, & Bove, 2006.)

Efficacy of Intervention with Adjudicated Males
Heads UP Men can be an integral part of any campus judicial system. Participation in a Heads UP Men judicial group is the sanction that first-time alcohol-related judicial offenders receive at LMU. Participants in the Heads UP Men judicial program demonstrated reductions in drinking, and consequently, a reduction in several negative consequences due to drinking. During Year 2 of the project, Heads UP Women was implemented for adjudicated female students. Prior to the inception of the women's program, Heads UP Men was the primary sanction for all judicially referred students, including women. The following table shows completion rates for participants by sex for Heads UP Men and Heads UP Women. Participants who did not complete three months of diaries were fined by the LMU Office of Judicial Affairs for not completing the project.

Table 1: Number of Participants & Diary Completion Rates

	Year 1 2003-2004	Year 2 2004-2005	Year 3 2005-2006
Heads Up Men Completion Rate	167 (100 male and 67 females) 96% (1mo); 84% (3mo)	84 (73 male and 11 female) 93% (1mo); 84% (3mo)	157 99% over 12 weeks
Heads Up Women Completion Rate		35 97% over 12 weeks	110 99% over 12 weeks

All 408 judicial participants drank within the past three months. At three-month follow-up, all judicial participants reduced their total drinks per month (quantity X frequency) by 37% from 67.75 drinks per month to 42.39 drinks per month. When compared by gender, both males and females benefited equally from the intervention. At the three-month follow-up, males reduced drinks per month by 36% from 72.29 drinks to 46.05, and women reduced drinks per month by 46% from 49.05 to 26.63 drinks (see Figure 4).

Figure 4: Outcomes for all judicial participants (Years 1 to 3)

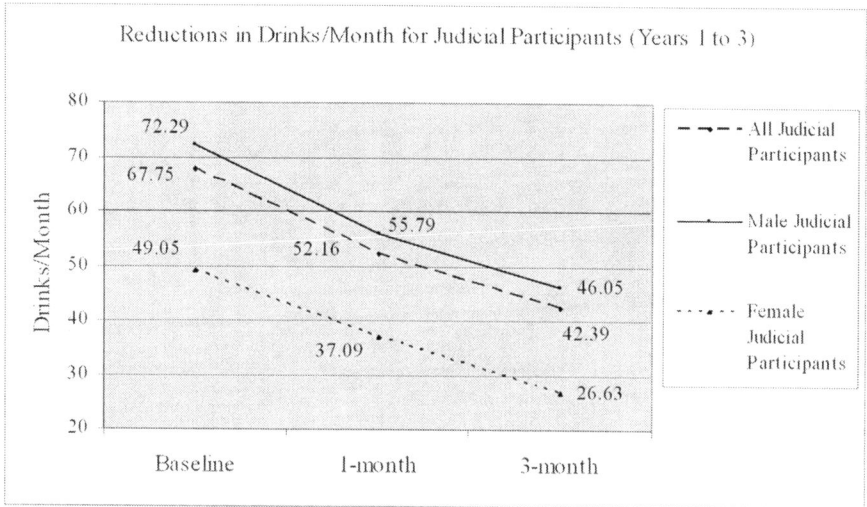

Reductions in Drinks/Month for Judicial Participants (Years 1 to 3)

© LaBrie, Lamb, Pedersen, & Quinlan, 2006

The following analyses highlight the findings found separately in Year 1 and Years 2 and 3 combined. Detailed results from Year 1 of the project can be found in LaBrie, Lamb, Pedersen, & Quinlan (2006) and results from Years 2 and 3 can be found in LaBrie, Pedersen, & Buckley, (in review). All results include students who drank at least once in the three months before the intervention and the three months after the intervention.

Year 1: Judicial Participants (n = 167)
Both male and female judicial participants reduced drinking. Males reduced drinks per month 50%, from 96.54 to 47.76 ($p < .001$), while females' total drinks reduced 45%, from 54.00 to 29.52 at follow-up ($p < .01$). Males reduced maximum drinks 43% from 15.40 drinks to 8.72 ($p < .001$), while females reduced maximum drinks 35% from 9.52 to 6.15 drinks ($p < .001$). Frequent binge drinkers (males and females) reported the sharpest reductions, with drinks per month decreasing 53% from 113.93 to 53.03 and maximum drinks 22% from 12.24 to 9.54.

Figure 5-I

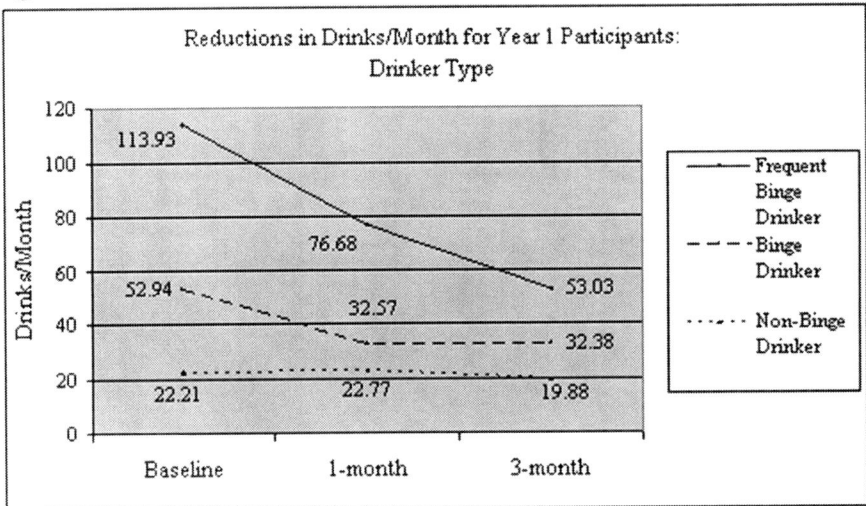

Reductions in Drinks/Month for Year 1 Participants:
Drinker Type

© LaBrie, Lamb, Pedersen, & Quinlan, 2006

Figure 5-II

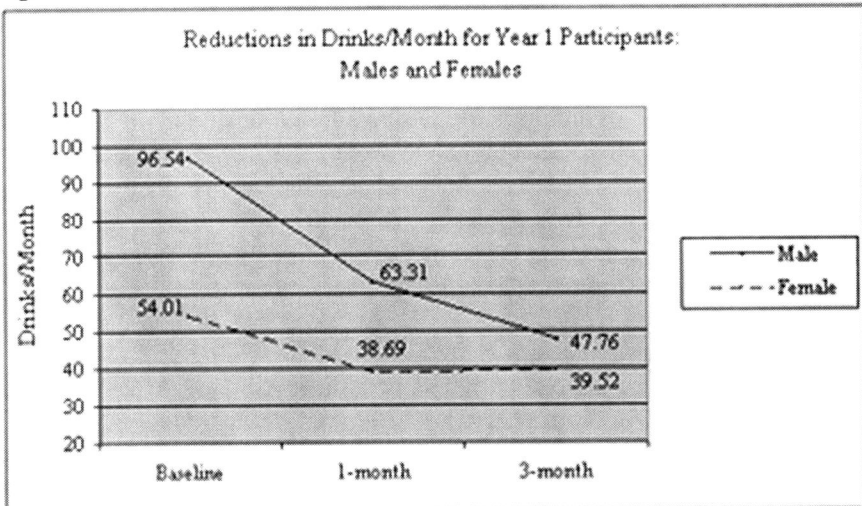

Reductions in Drinks/Month for Year 1 Participants:
Males and Females

(*Note: NBD = Non-binge drinkers; BD = binge drinker; FBD = frequent binge drinker*)
© LaBrie, Lamb, Pedersen, & Quinlan, 2006

All adjudicated participants also decreased the amount of alcohol-related problems (as determined by the RAPI) from pre-intervention to follow-up. Males and females had 65% and 49% fewer alcohol-related problems, respectively. Frequent binge drinkers had 68% fewer alcohol-related problems at follow-up. Finally, records from the Judicial Affairs Office revealed that 15% (*n* = 25) of the judicial participants received at least one additional alcohol-related sanction, significantly less than the greater than 50% recidivism rate reported by Friar (2002) prior to the inception of Heads UP.

Years 2 and 3: Judicial Participants (n = 241)
Due to the inception of Heads UP Women in fall semester of 2004, only 13 women attended the Heads UP Men groups during Year 2 and no women attended Heads UP Men groups during Year 3. Therefore, male and females are included in analyses. Judicial participants reduced drinks per month by 27% from 60.32 to 44.16 at three-month follow-up. Frequent binge drinkers reported sharpest reductions with drinks per month decreasing 34% from 87.74 to 58.14.

Figure 6-I

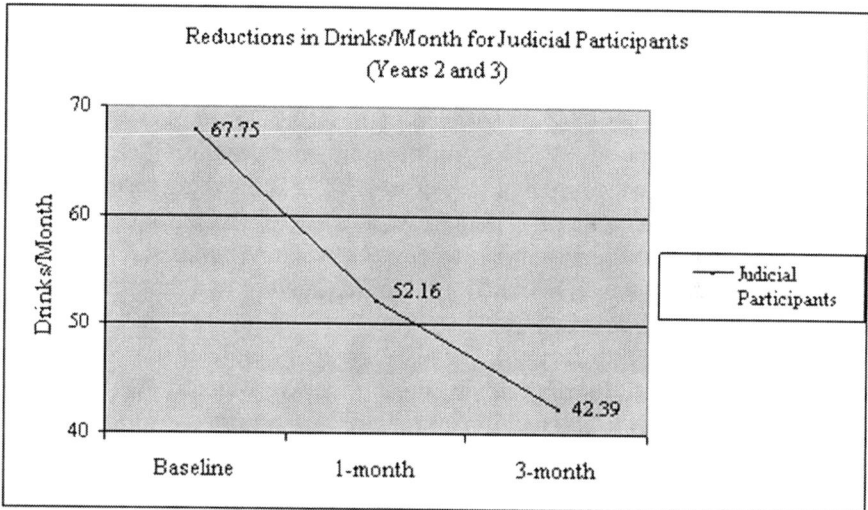

© LaBrie, Lamb, Pedersen, & Quinlan, 2006

Figure 6-II

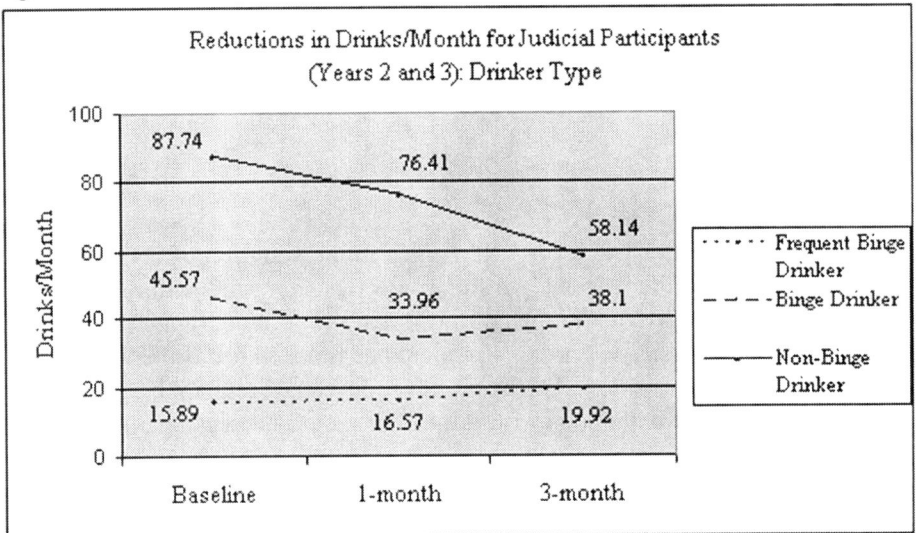

Reductions in Drinks/Month for Judicial Participants
(Years 2 and 3): Drinker Type

© LaBrie, Lamb, Pedersen, & Quinlan, 2006

All participants from Years 2 and 3 significantly reduced the amount of alcohol-related problems (as determined by the RAPI) from pre-intervention to three-month follow-up by 33%. Additionally, to determine if citation alone impacted drinking, we compared participants' TLFB drinking behavior with the date students were cited by Student Affairs staff for violating campus alcohol policies. The mean number of days between write-up and the intervention was 78.65 (SD = 41.97), or approximately two months. We found that simply being cited did not produce reductions in drinking (LaBrie, Pedersen, & Buckley, in review). Finally, university judicial records revealed a 10% recidivism rate for participants during the two years of the study (n = 24). This was similar to the recidivism rate of 15% reported during the first year of the study and much different from the rate reported before the implementation of the group-based BMI (59%). (Please note that Figures 4, 5, and 6 are originally cited in LaBrie, Lamb, Pedersen, & Quinlan, 2006).

Efficacy of Heads Up Women
Efficacy of the Intervention with Freshman Females
Following the success of the Heads UP Men program, the Heads UP Women program followed suit with excellent results. Consistent with hypotheses, there was a significant main effect for the intervention, as participants receiving the intervention drank fewer drinks per week, had fewer binge drinking episodes per month, and reported fewer alcohol consequences than assessment-only control participants.

Further, the intervention's effect was moderated by social and enhancement drinking motives such that women with high social and enhancement motives were more likely to experience an intervention effect than women with low social and enhancement motives for drinking. Thus, it appears that this targeted motivational enhancement intervention was effective in reducing drinking and risk associated with drinking among freshman women in their first semester at college.

Alcohol Consumption
There was a main effect for intervention indicating that across all 10 follow-up time points, participants in the intervention group drank fewer drinks per week than participants in the control group, $F(1,201) = 5.82, p < .05, d = .34$. Figure 1 contains means for intervention and control groups across all time periods adjusted for baseline drinks per week.

Figure 1

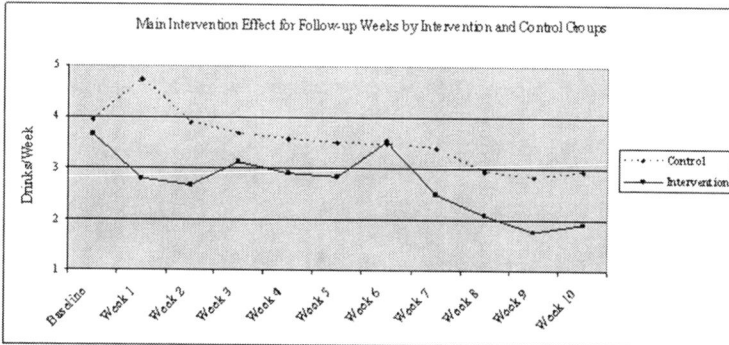

Main Intervention Effect for Follow-up Weeks by Intervention and Control Groups

© LaBrie, Tawalbeh, Huchting, Pedersen, Thompson, Neighbors, Shelesky, & Larimer, 2007

There was a main effect for intervention indicating that participants in the intervention group had fewer binge episodes in the month following the intervention and during weeks 7-10 than participants in the control group, $F(1,202) = 8.75, p < .01, d = .42$. Means and standard deviations at baseline for intervention and control groups, respectively, were 1.87 (2.85) vs. 1.85 (3.19), compared with four weeks at 1.40 (2.19) vs. 2.08 (3.57), and ten weeks at 1.08 (1.77) vs. 1.62 (2.94) (see Figure 2-I).

Alcohol-related Consequences
RAPI scores at four weeks and ten weeks were examined as a repeated measure and evaluated as a function of intervention group controlling for baseline RAPI scores. A main effect for intervention, $F(1,193) = 3.90, p = .05, d = .28$, suggested that consequences were lower post-intervention in the

intervention group compared to the control group. Means and standard deviations on the RAPI were 2.12 (3.04) vs. 2.35 (3.90) at baseline, 2.30 (3.34) vs. 2.97 (4.46) at four weeks, and 1.94 (3.10) vs. 2.76 (4.45) at ten weeks for the intervention and control groups, respectively (see Figure 2-II).

Figure 2-I

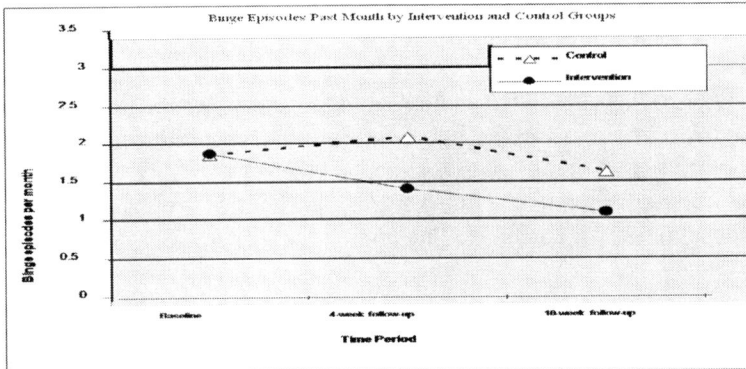

© LaBrie, Tawalbeh, Huchting, Pedersen, Thompson, Neighbors, Shelesky, & Larimer, 2007

Figure 2-II

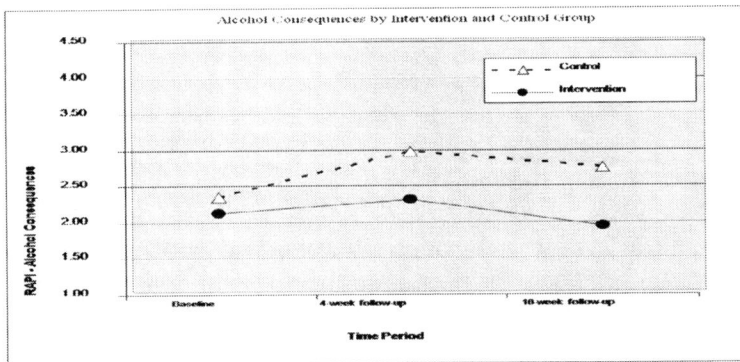

© LaBrie, Tawalbeh, Huchting, Pedersen, Thompson, Neighbors, Shelesky, & Larimer, 2007

An interaction was evident between social motives and intervention group for both drinks per week, $F (1,194) = 9.43$, $p < .001$, $d = .44$, and maximum drinks, $F (1,194) = 5.97$, $p < .05$, $d = .35$. Interactions were graphed and interpreted based on predicted cell means derived from parameter estimates as outlined by Aiken and West (1991). High and low values for social motives were defined as one standard deviation above and below the mean, respectively. Results suggest that the intervention effect was strongest among women with greater social motivations for drinking (see Figure 3). The interaction for maximum drinks paralleled that for drinks per week.

Figure 3: Social motives

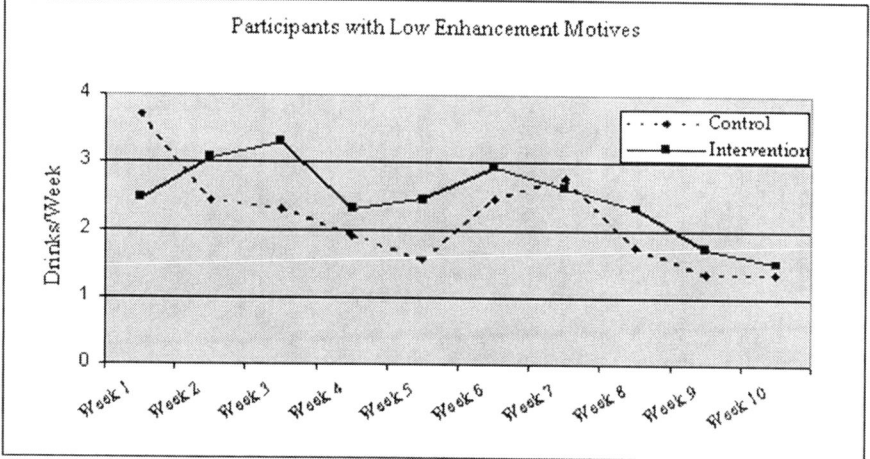

Participants with Low Enhancement Motives

©LaBrie, Tawalbeh, Huchting, Pedersen, Thompson, Neighbors, Shelesky, & Larimer, 2007

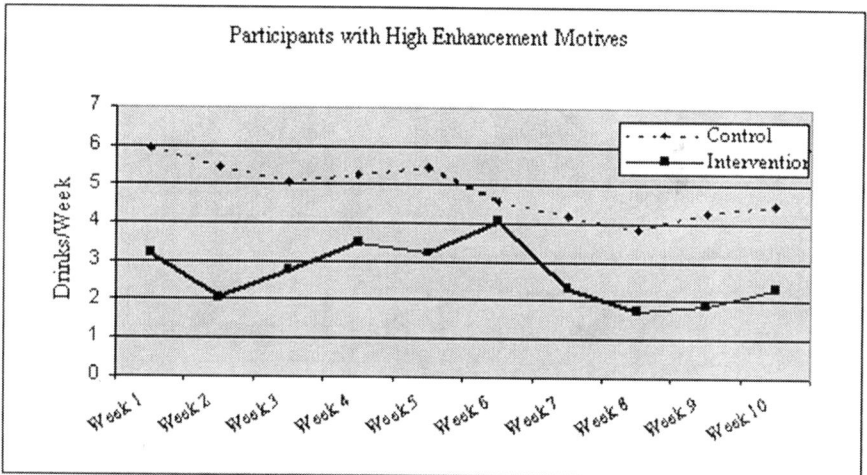

Participants with High Enhancement Motives

© LaBrie, Tawalbeh, Huchting, Pedersen, Thompson, Neighbors, Shelesky, & Larimer, 2007

Similarly, there was an interaction between enhancement motives and intervention group for both drinks per week, $F(1,194) = 5.73, p < .05, d = .34$, and maximum drinks, $F(1,194) = 5.37, p < .05, d = .33$. Interactions were graphed and interpreted as described above. The intervention was more effective among women with stronger enhancement drinking motives (see

Figure 4). Again, the interaction for maximum drinks was similar to that for drinks per week.

Figure 4: Enhancement motives

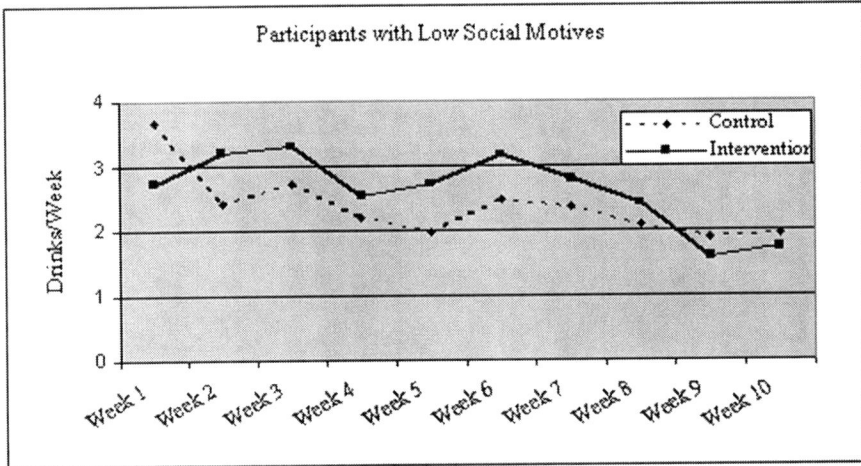

© LaBrie, Tawalbeh, Huchting, Pedersen, Thompson, Neighbors, Shelesky, & Larimer, 2007

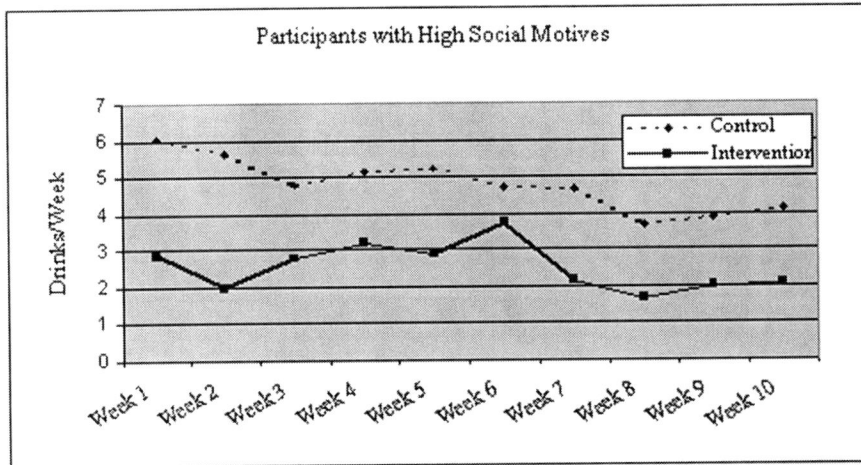

© LaBrie, Tawalbeh, Huchting, Pedersen, Thompson, Neighbors, Shelesky, & Larimer, 2007

In conclusion, this selective group prevention intervention targeting freshman female students was successful in preventing the establishment of heavy drinking patterns during the first semester of college, the most critical time according to the NIAAA. The utility of this intervention lies in the group design, which can reduce the drain on multiple university resources. The structure of the group dynamic specifically addresses reasons for drinking and issues relevant to college women. Other universities are encouraged to adopt similar targeted interventions on their own campuses to aid in preventing excessive alcohol use by college students, particularly first-year females. (Figures 1-4 are originally cited in LaBrie et al., 2007).

Efficacy of the Intervention with Adjudicated Females
During Year 2 of the project, 35 women participated in the Heads UP Women program. During Year 3 of the project, Heads UP Women became the primary first-line sanction for all sanctioned female students at the university. One hundred and ten women received the intervention during Year 3. Like the men, the sanction included 12 weeks of behavioral diaries. Participants who did not complete three months of diaries were fined by the LMU Office of Judicial Affairs for not completing the project.

All 150 judicial participants drank within the past three months. At three-month follow-up, all judicial participants reduced their total drinks per month (quantity X frequency) by 29% from 35.22 drinks per month to 25.04 drinks per month at three month follow-up (see Figure 5).

Figure 5

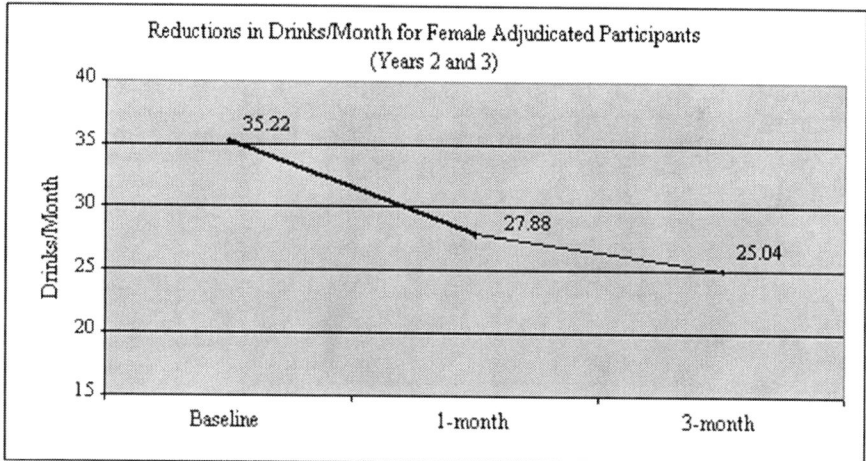

Reductions in Drinks/Month for Female Adjudicated Participants (Years 2 and 3)

The following analyses highlight the findings found among Heads UP Women during Year 3 of the project. The small number of participants during Year 2 makes it difficult to find meaningful or generalizable results among these participants. Detailed results from Year 3 are below.

Year 3: Judicial Participants (n = 110)
Female judicial participants reduced drinking over the three months of follow-up. Participants reduced drinks per month by 12% from 32.14 to 28.35 (*p* = .15) at one-month follow-up and by 26% to 23.87 (*p* < .01) at three-month follow-up. Frequent binge drinkers reported the sharpest reductions, with drinks per month decreasing 26% from 55.76 to 41.05.

Figure 6-I

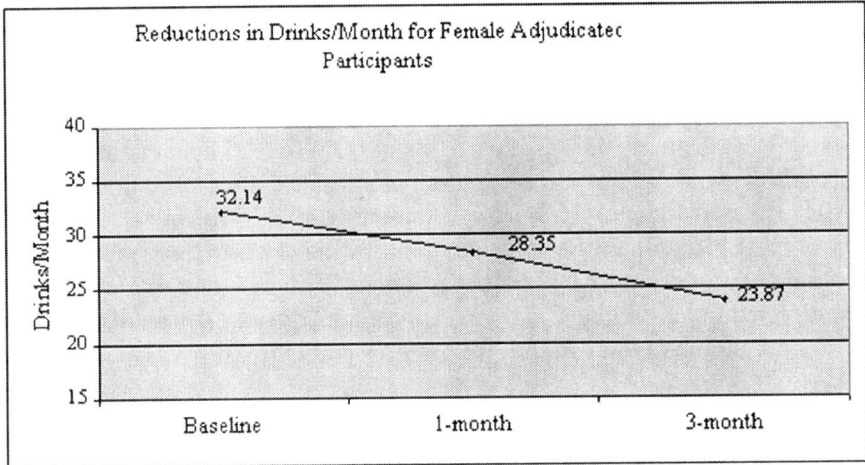

Reductions in Drinks/Month for Female Adjudicated Participants

Figure 6-II

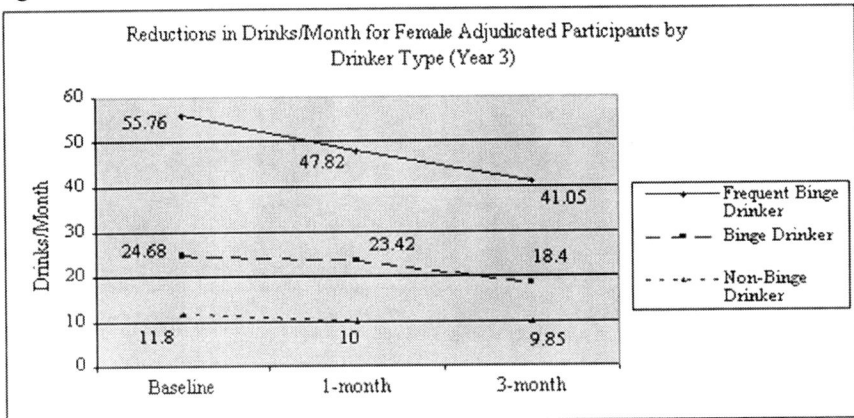

Reductions in Drinks/Month for Female Adjudicated Participants by Drinker Type (Year 3)

All adjudicated participants also decreased the amount of alcohol-related problems (as determined by the RAPI) from pre-intervention to follow-up. Participants experienced a 36% reduction in RAPI scores at three-month follow-up.

Chapter VI

Assessment, the Group Session, and Evaluation

Institutional Assessment

As mentioned previously, a thorough assessment of your university's or organization's needs, programs, and alcohol issues is essential prior to implementing Heads UP. The specific needs of your university or organization can guide the focus and administration of the Heads UP intervention.

The following are some suggested methods of assessment. After a thorough search of standardized measures used in the field, the following measures were chosen for use in the intervention at LMU. Bear in mind, this is not a comprehensive list, and it may be helpful to conduct a search for measures specific for your institution.

The CORE Alcohol and Drug Survey – Short Form

The CORE survey assesses alcohol and other drug use, attitudes toward drinking, and perceptions of social norms for college students. It contains 23 items, and administration takes approximately 10 minutes. This survey has demonstrated validity and reliability (CORE, 1989-1991).

Faculty and Staff Environmental Alcohol and Other Drug Survey

The Faculty and Staff survey assesses perceptions of alcohol and other drug use on campus, as well as general attitudes toward substance use, of faculty and staff on campus. The survey contains 41 items and takes approximately 20 minutes to complete. The measure is valid (content validity agreement rated by experts of .90) and reliable (Cronbach's alpha for survey of .81). The survey assesses five specific areas, including policy, prevention program awareness, involvement in prevention, assessment, and perception of problem (CORE, 1993).

The e-Chug

The e-Chug provides individual feedback regarding each individual's drinking. This brief assessment is available online or in paper form. The online version allows for immediate feedback regarding drinking patterns and normative drinking behaviors. Administration time is approximately 10-15 minutes. Although this assessment is aimed at providing personalized feedback as a form of intervention, normative information can also be extracted from the data (Steiner, Woodall, Yeagley, 2005; Van Sickle & Sokolow, 2006). As mentioned previously, the AUDIT is also included in this measure. The e-Chug has proven to be an effective intervention for problem drinking on campuses (Steiner, Woodall, & Yeagley; Walters, Matson, & Harris, 2005). In addition, when used in conjunction with alcohol programming and interventions in place on campuses, the e-Chug has improved treatment outcomes (Henry, Lange, & Wilson, 2004; Wilson, Henry, & Lange, 2005).

Review of Judicial Sanctions (for University Settings)

Working together with your Judicial Affairs department in the collection and analyses of data as well as the implementation of the judicial component of the Heads UP program is integral to the program's success. Judicial Affairs departments often have record-keeping and data protocols in place. Ideally, you would be able to work within the framework of an existing system. The following is a list of statistics that are extremely helpful and often can be obtained through your Judicial Affairs department:

1. Frequency of alcohol-related sanctions,
2. Level of sanction required for alcohol-related incidents,
3. Pertinent and unidentifiable demographic information of participants in the program, and
4: Recidivism rates for alcohol-related sanctions.

Review of Judicial Trends at Your Institution

If you are not currently working in a university, it is important to assess the statistics regarding the population with whom you're working. For example, obtain information regarding the frequency with which female teenagers are charged with *minor in possession* in your immediate geographic area when treating a young woman for substance abuse.

Pre-Intervention Assessment

Once participants have been assigned to the intervention, you may find it beneficial to gather baseline data on your specific participants. At LMU, we gather both alcohol-related information as well as additional moderating factors that may affect the intervention. If you are considering an in-depth evaluation of the Heads UP program at your institution, you may find it helpful to administer these measures. Below is a list of measures and questions asked in our pre-intervention questionnaire and references for those valid and published.

1. Typical demographic questions, such as age, sex, ethnicity, religion, residence
   location, year in school, and socioeconomic status.
2. Self-report alcohol use and sexual behavior over the past 30 days.
3. Intended drinking over the next 30 days.

4. Sexual behavior including age of first sexual intercourse, number of partners in lifetime and in the past three months, and condom usage while drinking.

5. Normative questions about participants' perceptions of their own and others' drinking behavior and attitudes.

6. The Rutgers Alcohol Problem Index (RAPI), a 23-item assessment of alcohol-related problems and negative consequences. (White & Labouvie, 1989). Towards the assessment of adolescent problem drinking. *Journal of Studies on Alcohol, 50,* 30-37.

7. The Drinking Motives Questionnaire (DMQ), a 20-item questionnaire that assesses drinking motives (including social motives, coping motives, enhancement motives, and conformity motives). Cooper, L. M. (1994). Motivations for alcohol use among adolescents: Development and validation of a four-factor model. *Psychological Assessment, 6,* 117-128.

8. The Alcohol Use Disorders Identification Test (AUDIT), a 10-item assessment including subscales on the amount and frequency of drinking, alcohol dependence, and problems caused by alcohol.

9. Saunders, J. B., Aasland, O. G., Babor, T. F., De la Fuente, J. R., & Grant, M. (1993). Development of the alcohol use disorders screening test (AUDIT). WHO collaborative project on early detection of persons with harmful alcohol consumption. II. *Addiction, 88,* 791-804.

10. A readiness to change ruler on a 10-point Likert scale. LaBrie, J. W., Quinlan, T., Schiffman, J., & Earleywine, M. (2005). Performance of alcohol and safer sex rulers compared to readiness to change questionnaires. *Psychology of Addictive Behaviors 19*(1), 112-115.

11. General Well-Being rulers assessing perceptions of tension, health, depression, and energy. Rated on a 10-point Likert scale. Dupuy, H. J. Self-representations of general psychological well-being of American adults. Paper presented at the American Public Health Association Meeting, Los Angeles, CA; 1978.

12. Alcohol Expectancy Questionnaire (AEQ-3), including eight subscales, social and physical pleasure, social enhancement/expressiveness, global positive change, sexual enhancement, power and aggression, tension reduction/relaxation, cognitive and physical impairment, and careless unconcern, assessed on 40 items. George, W. H., Frone, M. R., Cooper, M. L., Russell, M., Skinner, J. B., & Windle, M. (1995). A revised Alcohol Expectancy Questionnaire: Factor structure confirmation and invariance in a general population sample. *Journal of Studies on Alcohol, 56*(2), 177-185.

13. College Alcohol Problems Scale–Revised (CAPS-R), assessed on 8 items. Maddock, J. E., LaForge, R. G., Rossi, J. S., & O'Hare, T. (2001). The college alcohol problems scale. *Addictive Behaviors, 26,* 385 – 398.

14. Brief Young Adult Alcohol Consequences Questionnaire (B-YAACQ) consists of 24 items derived from the 48-item Young Adult Alcohol Consequences Questionnaire. Assesses the full range of the alcohol problems continuum from signs of excessive drinking to symptoms consistent with alcohol abuse and alcohol dependence. Kahler C. W., Strong D. R., & Read J. P. (2005). Toward efficient and comprehensive measurement of the alcohol problems continuum in college students: the Brief Young Adult Alcohol Consequences Questionnaire. *Alcoholism: Clinical & Experimental Research, 29,* 1180-1189. The Young Adult Alcohol Problems Screening Test (YAAPST), a 27-item assessment reviewing alcohol-related problems. Hurlburt, S. C., & Sher, K. J. (1992). Assessing alcohol problems in college students. *Journal of American College Health, 41,* 49-58.

15. Duke Health Profile, a 17-item generic self-report instrument containing six health measures (physical, mental, social, general, perceived health, and self-esteem), and four dysfunction measures (anxiety, depression, pain, and disability). Parkerson, G. R. Jr., Broadhead, W. E., & Tse, C. K. (1990). The Duke Health Profile. A 17-item measure of health and dysfunction. *Medical Care, 28,* 1056-1072.

Chapter VII

Heads UP Intervention Protocol

Welcome (5 minutes)

Overview
We begin the group session by thanking participants for attending. Even if this is a judicial group session, participants have the option of attending, and their decision to attend the session should be acknowledged. It is important to begin and carry on throughout the group using the Motivational Interviewing techniques. Specifically, in the introduction of the group it is important to realize that some participants may begin with an attitude of resistance. Meet these participants honestly; roll with their attitude. Let them express their opinion and acknowledge their feelings. This is particularly pertinent for judicial groups. State the objectives of the program clearly.

After thanking the participants for their attendance, it is important for the facilitators to introduce themselves, describe their role in the project, and provide any relevant information (e.g., whether or not the facilitator attended school at this institution or how long he or she has been working for the project). This introduction makes the facilitators real people and answers any questions the participants may have about who they are.

Participants are then asked what they have heard about the program. This is helpful for the facilitators to get the pulse of the experiences students have had or what they have heard about the program. Validate responses. This is where the stage is set for interaction. If participants do not respond, jump in and state clearly the role of the program, the objectives of the program, and the role of the participant in the program. The key point here is that you are here to learn from the participants. You want to know what it is like for them as a student at this university/college. Another point to stress is that this program is about general health and well-being, not only about alcohol.

Welcome and thank you for being here for the Heads UP Program.
What have you heard about this program?

Wait for a response, reflect the responses, and then explain what the program is about.

Briefly, Heads UP is a program with two functions: a long-term research project which you are all involved in and alcohol programming events on campus. In general, Heads UP is a program aimed at helping students make the best individual choices about their personal drinking behaviors as well as general health and well-being. We are not an abstinence-based program. Rather, we encourage mindfulness about decisions that affect health and well-being. Our purpose today is to learn more from you about college students and drinking.

Review of Informed Consent

Overview
The informed consent form allows participants to give consent to participate in the study. It outlines their concerns for confidentiality and explains the complete anonymity of their responses. In addition, the informed consent gives participants a brief synopsis of what will occur in the session and throughout the project. This way there are no surprises, and participants feel that they are in the loop.

Instructions

Please take a look at the form coming around. This is the informed consent form. It states that we will not share your information with anyone. It also provides a description of what will be covered in the group.

Your name will not be on any forms except the consent form and the sign-in sheet. You will use the sequence number we have provided you on all other forms.

We will keep all of your answers to the questionnaires confidential as well as anything you choose to share with the group today. What questions do you have about the forms or the group?

What you choose to share is up to you. We welcome everyone's opinions in our discussion today. If you choose to share today, that would be great, and it would be helpful if what will be shared in the room during the groups would stay in the room in order for everyone to feel comfortable. It is important to hear everyone's ideas and opinions and to share a mutual respect for one another in our different opinions. For example, we expect that some of you may drink and some of you may not drink.

Goal

The goal of the informed consent is to provide participants a brief description of what they will be participating in and what is expected of them. This document gives them the choice to participate.

*Note: The following pages consist of the three informed consent forms used in Heads UP at LMU. One is for female first-year volunteers and the other two are for male and female judicially-referred participants. It may be helpful to review these and modify them to fit your school's needs.

[Your University/Institution]
Informed Consent Form - Judicial
Heads UP Men

I hereby authorize the Heads UP program, directed by **[name of director]**, to include me in the Heads UP study.

I have been sanctioned to Heads UP as part of my judicial offense. The Heads UP program consists of a brief motivational enhancement group. I will also be asked to fill out a daily log for the three months following the first meeting. This log will ask me to check various behaviors that I have engaged in each day. The log should take no longer than five minutes a day and is to be completed online at an assigned website at the end of each month for the next three months. At the end of three months I will be asked to fill out and submit another brief questionnaire.

I will be asked to honestly explore issues around my drinking. I understand that Heads UP is completely separate from the Judicial Affairs Office and none of my responses will ever be given over to the Judicial Affairs Office for any use. Heads UP will coordinate all data collection and will only report to the Judicial Affairs Office whether or not I have completed each part of the program. Failure to complete all aspects of the program will result in being assigned a different judicial sanction by the Judicial Affairs Office. I am asked to enter this program as openly and honestly as I can, since no specific information about me will ever be given to the Judicial Affairs Office.

Prior to the motivational enhancement group I will be asked to fill out a questionnaire that inquires about my past alcohol-related behavior, my intended future alcohol-related behavior, and my attitudes, thoughts, and beliefs toward changing these behaviors. This should take no longer than 20-30 minutes.

In the group session, I will be asked to look back at my drinking behavior over the past 3 months. Then I will create a list of the pros and cons of changing my drinking behavior. These first four steps will be done at one time. They should take no longer than 1-1.5 hours.

I realize that I am participating in a study on my beliefs and thoughts I have about drinking in general and my own alcohol consumption.

I understand that there is no deception involved in this study. Furthermore, I will not be required to undergo any experience whatsoever beyond filling out the questionnaires, participating in the brief motivation enhancement group, and participating in the follow-up portions. Because alcohol use and sexual behavior are generally personal and private, I may experience some discomfort or embarrassment as a result of being asked about them. I understand that all of my responses are strictly anonymous and confidential. Also if I do not want my responses to be scored or used in this study, I may ask to have them eliminated from the study.

CONFIDENTIALITY AND ANONYMITY: I realize that I am also required to maintain my own absolute confidentiality in this study, which means: (1) With the exception of this informed consent form, I will not put my name or other identifying information on anything I turn in; (2) I will not disclose any information about other students that I receive in the course of the motivational enhancement group. I realize that if I violate these confidentiality requirements, I will be violating **[your institution]** student conduct and ethics policies, and I may be referred to Judicial Affairs. I understand there will be an arbitrarily assigned sequence number on all my questionnaires and drinking logs. The purpose of this sequence number is to keep track of materials collected in the study. Information regarding the participant's first name, contact information, participant ID number, and whether or not each aspect of the study has been completed will be kept locked in cabinets accessible to the principal investigator only, separate from the actual data at all times. This will ensure that the data provided from the study will always be associated with a participant ID number and will never be connected directly with any names or identifying information. Moreover, examination of the study data will focus on highlighting group trends, and no individual information will be divulged.

POTENTIAL BENEFITS TO SUBJECTS AND/OR TO SOCIETY: This study will not directly benefit me, except insofar as it helps me assess my own drinking behaviors and my own desire to change these behaviors. Alcohol-related problems continue to be major health issues for the U.S. at large and for young persons in particular. The intention of this study is that it will provide more information about alcohol behavior. This could help in developing better prevention campaigns. My responses may help give a clearer picture about how people go about changing behaviors that are directly related to their health.

I accept responsibility for my actions and any uncomfortable feelings that may result. If I feel uncomfortable due to my participation in this study I realize I may speak to the Heads UP personnel (see next paragraph) or I may speak to a professional counselor at **[name/location of on-campus or local mental health services]**.

[name of director] can be reached at **[location/phone/email]** if I have any questions or concerns about my participation in this study.

I understand that I may withdraw from this study at any time. However, if I choose to do so I will be assigned a different judicial sanction by the Judicial Affairs Office. I understand I have the right to refuse to answer any question that I may not wish to answer. I am not waiving any legal claims, rights, or remedies because of my participation in this research study. If I have questions regarding my rights as a research subject I may contact **[name of chair of IRB or name of director of program]** at **[location/phone/email]**.

In signing this consent form, I acknowledge a receipt of a copy of this form.

Participant's Signature:_____ Date:_____
Witness's Signature:_____

[Your University/Institution]
Informed Consent Form - Volunteer
Heads UP Women

I hereby authorize the *Heads UP Women* staff, directed by **[name of director]**, to include me in the *Heads UP Women* study. I realize that I am participating in a study that evaluates student perceptions of alcohol attitudes and behavior, and I will be asked about my own attitudes and behavior. I will also be presented with information regarding reducing risks I may experience from my own alcohol use. I will also be asked to fill out a brief daily diary for the ten weeks following the group session. This diary will ask me to report various behaviors that I have engaged in each day. The diary is submitted online at the end of each week, and at the end of ten weeks I will be asked to fill out a final brief questionnaire. I understand that I must be at least 18 years of age to participate in this study.

Heads UP Women consists of a single alcohol-related motivational focus group. Prior to the group session, I will be asked to fill out an online questionnaire that inquires about my past alcohol-related behavior, my intended future alcohol-related behavior, and my attitudes, thoughts, and beliefs toward changing these behaviors. This will take no longer than 20 to 30 minutes. During the group session, I will be asked to look back at my drinking behavior over the past three months. I will participate in a discussion on reasons for drinking and the influence of drinking in my life. We will discuss drinking norms here at LMU and the role of drinking in sexual assault and violence. In addition, an interactive discussion regarding the gender-specific health effects of alcohol will be presented. The group session should take no longer than 90-120 minutes.

I understand that there is no deception involved in this study. Furthermore, I will not be required to undergo any experience whatsoever beyond filling out the questionnaires, participating in the brief motivational enhancement group, and participating in the follow-up portions. Because alcohol use and sexual behavior are generally personal and private, I may experience some discomfort or embarrassment as a result of being asked about them. If I do not feel comfortable participating in discussions, I understand that I do not have to disclose any information that I do not wish to. I further understand that all of my responses are strictly anonymous and confidential. In addition, if I do not want my responses to be scored or used in this study, I may ask to have them eliminated from the study.

CONFIDENTIALITY AND ANONYMITY: **[If you have a Confidentiality Certificate, enter information here; if not, remove this section]** To help keep information about me confidential, Heads UP has obtained a Confidentiality Certificate from the Department of Health and Human Services (DHHS). The Confidentiality Certificate **[certificate #]** will protect the investigators from being forced, even under a court order or subpoena, to release information that could identify me. However, they may release identifying information in some circumstances. For example, they may disclose medical information in cases of medical necessity, or take steps (including notifying authorities) to protect me or someone else from serious harm, including child abuse.

I realize that I am also required to maintain my own absolute confidentiality in this study, which implies that: (1) I will not put my name or other identifying information on anything I complete; (2) I will not disclose any information about other students that I receive in the course of the motivational enhancement group; and (3) I realize that if I violate these confidentiality requirements, I will be violating **[your institution]** student conduct and ethic's policies.

I understand that I will be assigned an arbitrary sequence number to use on all of my questionnaires and drinking diaries. The purpose of this sequence number is to keep track of materials collected in the study. I understand that most of my responses will be collected through an online data collection program. All data collected online will be encrypted with my sequence number, so that no responses will be linked to any identifying information, including my name and email address. The encrypted data will be kept separate from another online file which contains names and email addresses. Information regarding the participants' first name, contact information, participant ID number, and whether or not each aspect of the study has been completed will be kept separate from the actual data at all times. Names and contact information will be kept in locked file cabinets and will be accessible by the principal investigator only. This will ensure that the data provided from the study will always be associated with a participant sequence number and will never be connected directly with any names or identifying information. Moreover, examination of the study data will focus on highlighting group trends and no individual information will be divulged.

POTENTIAL BENEFITS TO SUBJECTS AND/OR TO SOCIETY: Alcohol-related problems continue to be major health issues for the U.S. at large and for young persons in particular. The hope of this study is that it will provide more information about alcohol behavior. This could help in developing better prevention campaigns. My responses may help give a clearer picture about how people go about changing behaviors that are directly related to their own health. This study will not directly benefit me, except insofar as it helps me assess my own drinking behaviors and my own desire to change these behaviors.

PAYMENT FOR PARTICIPATION: **[This section will be different for you depending on funding]** I will be reimbursed for my time in participating in this study. I will receive $40 monetary compensation following completion of the online survey and group session. For returning follow-up material (daily drinking diaries completed weekly for ten weeks), I will receive $10 for each diary submitted. Lastly, for completion of the final questionnaire, which will be completed following submission of all diaries, I will receive $15. I may receive up to $155 for completing all parts of the study. I accept responsibility for my actions and any uncomfortable feelings that may result. If I feel uncomfortable due to my participation in this study I realize I may speak to the researchers (see next paragraph), or I may speak to a professional counselor at the Student Psychological Services located on the 2nd floor of the Burns Recreation Center; (310) 338-2868.

[name of director] can be reached at **[location/phone/email]** if I have any questions or concerns about my participation in this study.

I understand that I may withdraw from this study at any time. I understand I have the right to refuse to answer any question that I may not wish to answer. I am not waiving any legal claims, rights, or remedies because of my participation in this research study. If I have questions regarding my rights as a research subject I may contact **[name of chair of IRB or name of director of program]** at **[location/phone/email]**.

In signing this consent form, I acknowledge a receipt of a copy of this form.

Participant's Signature:_____ Date:_____

Witness's Signature:_____

[Your University/Institution]
Informed Consent Form - Judicial
Heads UP Women

I hereby authorize the *Heads UP Women* staff, directed by **[name of director]**, to include me in the *Heads UP Women* study. I have been sanctioned by the Judicial Affairs Office as a consequence of violating university alcohol policies. After being informed of my options regarding applicable judiciary sanctions, I have chosen to participate in the *Heads UP Women* Responsible Drinking Project. *Heads UP Women* consists of a single alcohol-related motivational focus group. I will also be asked to fill out a daily diary for the 12 weeks following the group. This diary will ask me to report various behaviors that I have engaged in each day. The diary is submitted online at the end of each week, and at the end of 12 weeks I will be asked to fill out a final brief questionnaire.

I will be asked to honestly explore issues around my drinking. I understand that *Heads UP Women* is completely separate from the Judicial Affairs Office, and none of my responses will ever be given over to the Judicial Affairs Office for any use. *Heads UP Women* will coordinate all data collection and will only report to the Judicial Affairs Office whether or not I have completed each part of the program. Failure to complete all aspects of the program will result in being assigned an alternative sanction as deemed appropriate by the Judicial Affairs Office. I am asked to enter this program as openly and honestly as I can, since no specific information about me will ever be given to the Judicial Affairs Office.

Prior to the group session, I will be asked to fill out an online questionnaire that inquires about my past alcohol-related behavior, my intended future alcohol-related behavior, and my attitudes, thoughts, and beliefs toward changing these behaviors. This will take no longer than 20-30 minutes.

During the motivational group session, I will be asked to look back at my drinking behavior over the past three months. I will participate in a discussion on reasons for drinking and the influence of drinking in my life. During the group session, I will participate in a discussion of drinking norms here at LMU and how the role of drinking on campus affects college women. In addition, an interactive discussion regarding the gender-specific health effects of alcohol will be presented. The group session should take no longer than 90-120 minutes.

I understand that there is no deception involved in this study. Furthermore, I will not be required to undergo any experience whatsoever beyond filling out the questionnaires, participating in the brief motivation enhancement group, and participating in the follow-up portions. Because alcohol use and sexual behavior are generally personal and private, I may experience some discomfort or embarrassment as a result of being asked about them. If I do not feel comfortable participating in discussions, I understand I do not have to disclose any information that I do not wish to. I understand that all of my responses are strictly anonymous and confidential.

Also if I do not want my responses to be scored or used in this study, I may ask to have them eliminated from the study.

CONFIDENTIALITY AND ANONYMITY: **[If you have a Confidentiality Certificate, enter information here; if not, remove this section]** To help keep information about you confidential, we have obtained a Confidentiality Certificate from the Department of Health and Human Services (DHHS). The Confidentiality Certificate **[certificate number]** will protect the investigators from being forced, even under a court order or subpoena, to release information that could identify you. However, we may release identifying information in some circumstances. For example, we may disclose medical information in cases of medical necessity, or take steps (including notifying authorities) to protect you or someone else from serious harm, including child abuse.

I realize that I am also required to maintain my own absolute confidentiality in this study, which means: (1) I will not put my name or other identifying information on anything I turn in; (2) I will not disclose any information about other students that I receive in the course of the motivational enhancement group. I realize that if I violate these confidentiality requirements, I will be violating **[your institution]** student conduct and ethics policies.

I understand that I will be assigned an arbitrary sequence number to use on all of my questionnaires and drinking diaries. The purpose of this sequence number is to keep track of materials collected in the study. I understand that most of my responses will be collected through an online data collection program. All data collected online will be encrypted with my sequence number, so that no responses will be linked to any identifying information, including my name and email address. The encrypted data will be kept separate from another online file which contains names and email addresses. Information regarding the participants' first name, contact information, participant ID number, and whether or not each aspect of the study has been completed will be kept separate from the actual data at all times. Names and contact information will be kept in locked file cabinets and will be accessible by the principal investigator only. This will ensure that the data provided from the study will always be associated with a participant sequence number and will never be connected directly with any names or identifying information. Moreover, examination of the study data will focus on highlighting group trends and no individual information will be divulged.

POTENTIAL BENEFITS TO SUBJECTS AND/OR TO SOCIETY: Alcohol-related problems continue to be major health issues for the U.S. at large and for young persons in particular. The hope of this study is that it will provide more information about alcohol behavior. This could help in developing better prevention campaigns. My responses may help give a clearer picture about how people go about changing behaviors that are directly related to their own health. This study will not directly benefit me, except insofar as it helps me assess my own drinking behaviors and my own desire to change these behaviors.

I accept responsibility for my actions and any uncomfortable feelings that may result. If I feel uncomfortable due to my participation in this study, I realize I may speak to the Heads UP personnel (see next paragraph), or I may speak to a professional counselor at **[name/location of on-campus or local mental health services]**.

[Name of director] can be reached at **[location/phone/email]** if I have any questions or concerns about my participation in this study.

I understand that I may withdraw from this study at any time. However, if I choose to do so I will be assigned a different judicial sanction by the Judicial Affairs Office. I understand I have the right to refuse to answer any question that I may not wish to answer. I am not waiving any legal claims, rights or remedies because of my participation in this research study. If I have questions regarding my rights as a research subject, I may contact **[name of chair of IRB or name of director of program]** at **[location/phone/email]**.

In signing this consent form, I acknowledge a receipt of a copy of this form.

Participant's Signature:_____ Date:_____
Witness's Signature:_____

Initial Questionnaire (10 Minutes)

Overview
The initial questionnaire consists of several developed, revised, and validated questionnaires about drinking behavior and drinking-related attitudes and beliefs. Feel free to develop your own questionnaire if you wish to evaluate the effectiveness of your program.

This portion of the program can be completed online if the proper equipment is obtained. Participants can be emailed this questionnaire and asked to fill it out and bring it with them to the group meeting. If surveys are completed online, ask participants if they had any questions regarding the survey. Then continue to the Timeline Followback (TLFB) section. Make sure to review standard drinks, either during the initial question (if completed in the group) or during the TLFB (if the initial questionnaire was completed online).

Instructions

First, ask participants if they know the definition of "one standard drink."

One standard drink is considered a 12 oz. beer, a 1.25 oz. shot, a 4 oz. glass of wine, or a mixed drink containing a 1.25 oz. shot of alcohol. Not all mixed drinks contain exactly one shot (or comprise exactly one standard drink). For example, a Long Island Iced Tea has four shots in it and therefore would be considered four standard drinks; the equivalent of four cans of beer. Answer all questions in terms of standard drinks. Are there any questions about standard drinks before we proceed?

Goal
The goal of this questionnaire is for the researchers to gain a better understanding of the drinking patterns and beliefs about drinking of the students on this campus.

Timeline Followback Calendaring of Drinking Behavior (20 Minutes)

Overview
The Timeline Followback (TLFB) serves as a way to collect fairly accurate data about individual drinking behavior over the past three months.

Although it is meant to be an assessment tool, the TLFB can aid as a piece of the intervention by allowing participants to see and reflect on their drinking behavior over the past three months in a way they may never have done before.

Instructions
Facilitator Dialogue:
If it's okay with all of you, we're going to start today with an activity by calendaring the drinking and the non-drinking you've done over the past three months. Together, we are going to come up with how much alcohol you consumed on each day during the past three months. At first this may seem difficult, but if you use a calendar like this one [show the calendar], you will be surprised at how well you can remember your drinking days and patterns. A calendar is very useful in helping people recall their drinking.

Now let's begin. Let's start with yesterday and go back about three months. Please circle yesterday and go back three months from yesterday and circle that day [announce the date aloud]. Cross off the days from today on and the days before three months ago.

Mark these dates on the calendars and cross out dates outside of the three-month period.
As you can see, standard holidays are already marked for you on the calendar to help you recall your activities around these times. What are some other significant dates that have occurred in the past three months? What are some other big on-campus events that you can remember?

Encourage the use of a personal appointment book or daily diary to aid recall.

Facilitator Dialogue:
Now, come up with any other special events or holidays that have occurred in the past three months that would help your memory. These can be good things or not-so-good things that have happened to you: birthdays, celebrations, hospitalizations, check receipt days, and so on. They can be related to drinking, or they can just be other memorable days that have occurred in the past month. We will call these "Marker Days." Fill out your own marker days on your calendars. You can use any marks you want to indicate your marker days; it is irrelevant for us to know what they are. They are simply going to be used to help you remember your drinking and non-drinking.

The idea here is to record the number of drinks you consumed each day. You will go back through each day of the calendar and write the number of standard drinks you consumed on each day. If you had no drinks on a day, mark a zero on that day.

It is important to record your drinking on the calendar in terms of standard drinks. What makes up one standard drink?

One standard drink is equal to one 12 oz. regular beer (a can or a bottle), one 4 oz. glass of wine, one 1.25 oz. shot of hard alcohol (like vodka or whiskey), one mixed drink with one 1.25 oz. shot of hard alcohol, a 10 oz. wine cooler, or an 8 oz. malt liquor.

What kinds of drinks do you normally have? How many standard drinks are included? For example, if you had a 40 oz. bottle of malt liquor, you would indicate that you drank about five standard drinks (malt liquor is higher in alcohol content than regular beer). Likewise, if you drank a Long Island Iced Tea with four shots of liquor in it, you would have had four standard drinks. A 12 oz. can of beer would be one standard drink. An "adios" would include about five standard drinks. What questions do you have about standard drinks?

Now, we are going to go back through the calendar every day for the past three months and mark what days you drank and how much you drank. Keep in mind this does not have to be perfect. We want you to be as accurate as possible, but we realize that it is hard for anyone to recall things perfectly. So if you can't recall, for example, whether you drank on a Monday or a Thursday of a certain week, just give it your best guess.

The same applies to quantity of drinks—just give it your best guess. If you don't remember whether you had 20, 21, or 22 drinks, put 21; 8, 9, or 10 drinks, put 9; or 2, 3, or 4 drinks, put 3; just choose the middle of the range. If you didn't drink at all, mark a zero on that day. What questions do you have?

For now, we are going to start with today and go back through each day of the last two weeks together. You will write the number of drinks you drank on each day that you drank.

We will walk around and help you while filling these out. Remember, this doesn't need to be perfect, but please try and be as accurate and honest as possible. Make sure to put down a single number for the amount of drinks, not a range. If you can't remember, just use your best guess. Then if it makes sense, you can continue to fill out the rest of the three months on your own.

Starting with yesterday, go back over the past month and indicate on which drinking days you believe you drank four drinks in one sitting (or five drinks for men). Indicate those days by circling the day.

Then ask participants to write a capital letter M on the day they drank the most.

Facilitator Dialogue:
Also, write "M" on the day you drank the most in the past month. If it seems reasonable, we can talk about this later on today.

When you are done, please write your participant ID number at the top of the calendar, flip it over, then pass it to one of us. Now that you have finished the calendar, what did you notice about your drinking behavior over the past three months?

Goal
The goal of the TLFB is to collect presumably accurate data on each drinking event over the course of a three-month period. This is preferable to single item self-reports of drinking behavior. From this assessment, many drinking variables can be created (such as drinking days per month; average drinks; maximum drinks consumed at one time; drinks per week; etc.) and used to measure change against follow-up data. An additional goal of the TLFB is to provide participants with a retrospective look at their drinking patterns and behavior in order to make them more aware of their own drinking before they compare it to their peers' drinking, and to help individuals to personally confront their own drinking patterns. Furthermore, the TLFB activity primes the students to remember their recent drinking behavior and helps to begin the process of assessing change.

Heads UP

Introductions (5 Minutes)

Overview
Introductions by both the facilitator and the participants help to reinforce the non-confrontational aspect of the group by reducing resistance and promoting honesty throughout the group session.

Instructions
The first facilitator begins, and then introductions are opened up to participants, and the second facilitator ends. If you feel the group is tired or particularly quiet, ask them how they feel about being in the session.

Facilitator Dialogue:
For judicial participants: Let's now take a moment to introduce ourselves to each other. Please state your first name, your year, where you live, how you ended up here (in Heads UP), and how you feel about being here.

For volunteer participants: Let's now take a moment to introduce ourselves to each other. Please state your first name, where you live, and where you're from.

Be mindful to be non-judgmental and non-confrontational with the participants. If a participant talks for too long and is just complaining about the reason he or she was written up, use MI techniques to turn the conversation around. Also, if a participant is upset about attending the session or feels that he or she should not be there, roll with her or his resistance and acknowledge the stated feelings. This will help to reduce resistance. If you counter the resistance or argue with the participant, it will only increase resistance.

Goal
This is a way to break the ice and put all participants on equal ground. For volunteer participants, the introduction is a way to identify themselves within the group. For judicial participants, it is important to give them time to voice their concerns about being sanctioned to attend the group. Most believe that they were "doing nothing wrong" and that their sanction was unfair. By listening and providing simple reflections, participants see that they can trust the facilitators to not reveal anything to Judicial Affairs, and this relaxed atmosphere helps facilitate comfort in the group discussions.

Good Things and Not-so-good Things about Drinking Discussion – Designed for Women's Groups (5 Minutes)

Overview
This is a brief discussion for students to get the group focused on the topic at hand. In addition, this discussion is meant to lead into the next section, where we will discuss expectancies regarding alcohol.

Instructions

When facilitating this discussion, it is important to remember to be brief. If a student continues talking for an extended period of time, lead the group in another direction. Try not to let the group fixate on one particular topic; instead, touch on the many good things and not-so-good things about drinking. Later in the session you will facilitate a more in-depth discussion of the reasons for drinking and not drinking. This discussion is very straightforward.

Facilitator Dialogue:
We'd like to ask you about the good things and the not-so-good things about drinking. What are the things you enjoy about drinking?

What are the not-so-good things about drinking?

Let participants briefly comment on issues around alcohol that are most salient for them. This section is an introduction to the topic, rather than an exhaustive list and discussion. The following are some examples as generated by previous groups; however, the content of the discussion should be generated by participants.

Facilitator Dialogue:
Good Things about Drinking: *Fun; social; feel more confident; feel more outgoing; gives me something to do; calms me down; it's exciting; it tastes good; it's available; why not?; makes me feel sexy; makes me feel more attractive; helps me bond with people; helps me have honest discussions; helps me cope with things; helps me forget; it's a thrill!*

Not-so-good Things about Drinking: *Interferes with studying for midterms; increases conflict; isn't compatible with my busy schedule; makes me gain weight; bad for my health; hangovers; spend too much money on alcohol; interferes with my religion; bad things have happened to me when I drank; I lost someone/something important to me; interferes with my grades; I become a different person; I get a bad reputation; I'm not able to meet new people; I can do harm to myself or someone else; people can get mean; I have regrets.*

Wrap up with content shared during the discussion: some of the good things were this and some of the not-so-good things were this. In doing this, we recap all of the things participants discussed about drinking.

Goal
The goal of the "Good Things/Not-so-good Things" discussion is to prepare participants for what is to come and to get them thinking about how they personally feel about drinking. Also, it helps participants to become aware of other participants' perceptions, hopefully creating an atmosphere that is open to diverse opinions. While the "Good Things/Not-so-good Things" discussion is designed for women, it may be used in men's sessions as well.

Expectancy Challenges (5 Minutes)

Overview
The goal of this discussion is to reduce positive drinking expectancies and to increase alternative explanations for enhanced sociability and sexual feelings in situations involving alcohol.

Instructions
If participants have addressed social issues of drinking during the previous discussion, use their responses here. If you chose not to conduct the previous discussion, you may prompt social expectations of alcohol use. For example, ask participants what social effects of alcohol they have noticed. Also, you may ask participants to guess the answers to the following questions. These data were obtained from the 2005 CORE survey.

Facilitator Dialogue:
What percentage of LMU students feel alcohol helps break the ice with people?
(82%)
What percentage of LMU students feel alcohol enhances social life?
(80%)
What percentage of LMU students feel alcohol helps facilitate sexual opportunities?
(63%)

Use this response if participants did not address social issues or there was no "Good Things/ Not-so-good Things" discussion:

Facilitator Dialogue:
These statistics tell us that many LMU students believe that alcohol affects us socially. Many people believe that alcohol makes them feel more outgoing, confident, friendlier, more gregarious, and more flirtatious.

If participants did address social issues in the "Good Things/Not-so-good Things" discussion:

Facilitator Dialogue:
You have mentioned that alcohol has many social effects linked with it. Many people believe that alcohol makes them feel more social, outgoing, confident with others, friendlier, more gregarious, and more flirtatious.

This is a topic that has interested many researchers, and we would like to share with you some of their findings. In order to study the effects of alcohol, researchers thought it would be best to create a situation around drinking that seemed the most real to college students. They created a bar lab, where students over 21 could drink and be monitored regarding the effects of alcohol on their behavior. As you can see in the following pictures, the lab was equipped with a two-way mirror, a microphone located in the top right corner, and a video camera hidden inside the Dos Equis sign.

In these studies, there were four groups. The groups included the various combinations of the following: alcohol vs. placebo and expected alcohol vs. didn't expect alcohol (draw graph to illustrate). The results were always the same.

Now at this time, it is appropriate for you to walk up to the PowerPoint chart (or a written chart on a white board) displaying the four conditions and point out the different conditions. Start with the two control conditions, in which participants get what they expect to get, and then ask what they think happened for the experimental/placebo conditions. Be very clear that the four conditions occurred at different times and not all four conditions in the room at the same time.

Expect

	Alcohol	No Alcohol
Receive / **Alcohol**	Person receives what he or she expects to (alcohol).	Person receives alcoholic beverage when expecting a non-alcoholic one.
No Alcohol	Person receives non-alcoholic beverage when expecting alcohol.	Person receives what he or she expects (non-alcoholic beverage).

For those who expected alcohol, regardless of whether they received alcohol or not, they were more gregarious, outgoing, loud, and social. For those who didn't expect alcohol, regardless of whether they received alcohol or not, they acted less social, less outgoing, and quieter. In fact, those who received alcohol and didn't expect it attributed the physiological effects, such as feeling warmer and more sleepy, to other things in their lives, such as high room temperature and not getting enough rest the night before, respectively. What do you all make of this?

Wait for students to interact with you and each other and provide responses. Highlight the role of what people expect with regard to their drinking behavior. Share how social and interpersonal aspects have more to do with expectations and mindset and less to do with the properties of alcohol. The physiological effects of the alcohol still occur, but not the social and interpersonal reactions. People expect alcohol to make them feel a certain way, so they in fact feel that way. It is the power of mind over physiology, much like the placebo effect. Ask participants, "What are some of the ways to experience the social aspect without alcohol?" If someone drinks to be funny or more outgoing, it is not actually the alcohol that is helping him or her but his or her expectation. Maybe ask how they think people felt when they were told they didn't get alcohol.

Facilitator Dialogue:
The big idea about expectancies is that they are important and they influence how we behave. The purpose of these questions was to help you figure out how you expect alcohol to affect you, and to be aware of these when you drink. Next time you are drinking, think, "What do I expect will result from my drinking?" and think about whether it is actually the alcohol or simply just you (your personality, your social skills) that is allowing these expectations to happen.

Goal

The goal of this section is to reduce positive drinking expectancies and to increase alternative explanations for enhanced sociability in situations involving alcohol. Also, with this section we hope to increase awareness of each individual's reasons for drinking and the effects that alcohol has on him or her.

Normative Data Feedback (15 Minutes)

Overview

Campus-specific normative feedback (based on the 2005 CORE survey) is presented to correct overestimations of perceived normative drinking. The group estimates alcohol use on campus and incidence rates for alcohol involvement in negative events (sexual assaults, violence, etc.), and they are provided with actual rates, giving students a snapshot of alcohol's role in negative events. Here we use campus-specific and gender-specific norms, as they appear to be more salient for participants. Please note that LMU data is provided. It would be beneficial for you to replace the LMU statistics with statistics either from your own institution, or national statistics. In addition, the same questions do not have to be used, but it is suggested that similar ones be posed.

Instructions

1. Provide participants with accurate and up-to-date information about actual drinking norms on campus using the 2005 CORE survey results. Ask participants what they think the statistics are and have them call out what they perceive it to be. After each response from participants, tell them the actual statistic.

2. If participants refute the norms, roll with their resistance. Acknowledge their thoughts that they do not believe the statistics or that they think those who took the survey were lying. Try different MI techniques to diffuse the resistance. One thing you may want to say is, "Did you lie while taking the survey?" or "It just seems like everyone is not truthful." One of the

reasons they do not believe the actual norm is because they do not know anyone who drinks like the norm. Ask them why this is. Often participants will say that it is not what they see; they see people intoxicated all the time, every day of the week. Acknowledge this and then reiterate that maybe those people they are surrounded by are not the norm, and they may seem to drink more. Also, point out that oftentimes we only recognize the outrageous cases. We give a lot of attention to the people who are not the norm. You may also want to tell them that there are many students on campus and that there will be some who drink like them, some who drink less than them, and some who drink more than them. This is a representative average of all students on campus.

3. If campus-specific statistics are not available, use national statistics.
4. This is often a fun section for participants. Allow them to be interactive.
5. This section often affords a great opportunity to highlight discrepancies in perceived norms and actual norms.
6. Below are sample statistics from LMU. When collecting baseline data, it may be helpful to ask similar questions or to use some of the measures previously suggested. Also, statistics are provided for males and females separately, and for students in general. It is helpful to provide sex-specific statistics in order to more fully engage students and make the information more salient.

Facilitator Dialogue:
Let's take a look at what you think drinking is like here at LMU. I will ask you some questions and I want you to guess what the answers are. The data provided is from the CORE survey administered to about 1,300 LMU students, with equal representation from each class (about 320 students from each class) in the spring of 2005.

1. *Think of all of the students at LMU...What percentage of all students drink two or less days per week?*
   - *89% of all LMU students drink two or less days per week (11% of all students drink three or more days per week). Think of all of the female students at LMU...What percentage of all female students drink two or less days per week?*
   - *94% of females (6% of female students drank three or more days per week; 8% for women drinkers only).*
     Think of all of the male students at LMU...What percentage of all male students drink two or less days per week?
   - *81% (19% of male LMU students drank three or more days per week).*

2. *What percentage of LMU students report drinking less than four drinks during a typical drinking occasion? (They were asked, "How much do you typically drink when you do drink?")*
   - *58% of students drank three or less drinks on average when drinking. What*
     percentage of LMU female students report drinking less than five drinks during a
     typical drinking occasion?
   - *66% of females drank three or less drinks on average when drinking (not bingeing).*
     What percentage of LMU students report drinking less than five drinks during a typical drinking occasion?
   - *54% of males drank four or less drinks on average when drinking.*

3. *What percentage of LMU students drank 15 or less drinks over the course of a typical week?*
   - *94% of LMU students drank 15 or less drinks over the course of a typical week at school.*
   What percentage of LMU female students drank 15 or less drinks over the course of a typical week?
   - *92% of LMU female students drank nine or less drinks over the course of a typical week at school.*
   What percentage of LMU male students drank 15 or less drinks over the course of a typical week?
   - *86% of LMU male students drank 15 or less drinks over the course of a typical week at school.*

4. *What percentage of LMU students report drinking six times per year or less?*
   - *30% of LMU students reported drinking six times a year or less.*
     What percentage of female LMU students report drinking six times per year or less?
   - *35% of LMU female students reported drinking six times a year or less.*
     What percentage of male LMU students report drinking six times per year or less?
   - *25% of LMU male students reported drinking six times a year or less.*

5. *What do you think is the average number of drinks consumed per week by LMU students?*
   - *4.5 drinks for all students*
     What do you think is the average number of drinks consumed per week by LMU female students?
   - *2.91 drinks per week for women*

What do you think is the average number of drinks consumed per week by LMU male students?
- *7.46 drinks for men*

6. *In the past month, what do you think is the average maximum amount of drinks the typical LMU student consumed at one time?*
   - *5.36 for all students*
     In the past month, what do you think is the average maximum amount of drinks the typical LMU female student consumed at one time?
   - *3.98 drinks at one time for women*
     In the past month, what do you think is the average maximum amount of drinks the typical LMU male student consumed at one time?
   - *7.79 drinks at one time for men*

What does your drinking look like? You might want to think about where you fall in comparison to the averages and what your drinking is like in comparison to your peers here at LMU.

Now if it's cool with you, we are going to talk about how drinking affects sexual experiences here at LMU.

Here, we can highlight some of those discrepancies and help participants realize where they fall within the campus norms.

7. *What percentage of the time is alcohol involved in the following experiences here at LMU? Students reported on the questionnaire that they experienced some sort of incident and then were asked if alcohol was involved when they experienced each incident. So, this is the percentage of the time that these incidences were reported in which alcohol was involved. These stats are for all students, including women, and are important for you to be aware of.*
- *Forced/unwanted sexual touching (i.e., being groped) (64%)*
- *Regretted sexual intercourse (76%)*
- *Unwanted sexual intercourse (i.e., rape) (80%)*

Goal
Providing participants with accurate, campus-specific norms helps correct their misperceptions of normative drinking patterns of students on their campus and nationally.

The Processing of Alcohol – Designed for Women's Groups (5 minutes)

Overview
As we mentioned previously in this manual, there are several key differences in the physiology of men and women that determines how alcohol affects them. The point of this discussion is to address those differences and make it clear to female participants why drinking for them is different from drinking for men.

Instructions
Begin by asking participants how drinking affects men and women differently. You will get many different responses. Some may say that women are more emotional, and men are more aggressive. While this may be generally true, we are more interested in the physiological differences. Affirm their responses and wait for more responses. Once a participant touches on a physiological difference or on one of the three factors that affect women differently than men, affirm the response, and continue with the three factors. Also, a participant may say that men are bigger and can therefore drink more. If this occurs, affirm the response, and then ask *"What if you hold size constant, and you have a man and a woman of the same size and weight?"*

Facilitator Dialogue:
How does alcohol affect men and women differently?

Women become intoxicated after drinking smaller quantities of alcohol than are needed to produce intoxication in men. So, even when size is comparable, there are still differences. This is due to three factors:

First, women have lower total body water content than men of comparable size. After alcohol is consumed, it diffuses uniformly into all body water, both inside and outside cells. Women and men are built differently. The average female carries more body fat than the average male (regardless of women's body structure), and thus less water, because body fat contains little water. Consequently, most women have less body water to dilute the alcohol, leaving a higher concentration of alcohol in their bodies. If you are drinking with a male friend, the same amount of alcohol you two drink is being processed more slowly for you than it is for him.

Second, alcohol dehydrogenase is a metabolizing enzyme in the stomach that helps the body get alcohol out of the system. Women have less of this enzyme than men, so more of what women drink enters the bloodstream as pure alcohol.

Third, women are susceptible to the intoxicating effects of alcohol when their estrogen levels are higher, both premenstrually and when taking birth control pills. There is evidence that women taking birth control pills will absorb alcohol faster, causing the intoxicating effects of alcohol to set in with smaller amounts of alcohol. In short, women get drunk more quickly and will stay intoxicated longer. Women absorb and metabolize alcohol differently than men. What effects that we spoke about have you noticed?

Here, the intention is to hear from participants their own experiences and make the discussion more salient to them.

Facilitator Dialogue:
What do you think about a situation where a woman and a man go drink for drink or shot for shot?

This question addresses the unfair disadvantage that women have when it comes to drinking.

Next, address the general physiological effects of alcohol. Participants will most likely say that alcohol affects the kidney and/or liver. Affirm these responses and then wait for a participant to bring up the depressant effects of alcohol; he or she may say alcohol slows the body down. If no participant gives this type of response, go into the explanation.

Facilitator Dialogue:
How does alcohol affect your body physiologically?

Wait for participants to respond. Affirm all true responses, and wait until someone says something related to the brain shutting down, e.g., loss of motor coordination, effects on thinking and decision making, or feeling dizzy.

Facilitator Dialogue:
Have you heard of some drugs classified as stimulants and other drugs classified as depressants?

Alcohol is interesting because, although it is a depressant drug, it can make people feel "revved up" initially by shutting down different circuits in the brain. When we say the word "depress" we actually mean to slow down. Yet, alcohol is a depressant that initially has stimulating effects.

You can only get to a certain level of feeling good before the depressant effects of alcohol kick in.

Next, if it's okay with you, let's address specific levels of alcohol in your body by addressing your own personal blood alcohol content.

Goal
The goal of this section is to help women become aware that alcohol affects their bodies differently than it does men's bodies. Also, it is important to have a general understanding of the effects of alcohol on the body in order to be more mindful when drinking.

Blood Alcohol Content (BAC) Discussion (5 Minutes)
Overview
Participants receive a personalized BAC card specific to their gender and weight. This information helps participants better understand how alcohol affects their bodies and teaches them to maximize the "good" things about consuming alcohol rather than experience the "not-so-good" things.

Instructions
Begin by passing out the BAC cards. While the participants are selecting the appropriate card, begin explaining the cards and what BAC is.

Blood Alcohol Concentration for Males

Weight	Number of drinks consumed per hour								
	1	2	3	4	5	6	7	8	9
100	.04	.08	.11	.15	.19	.23	.26	.30	.34
120	.03	.06	.09	.12	.16	.19	.22	.25	.28
140	.03	.05	.08	.11	.13	.16	.19	.21	.24
160	.02	.05	.07	.09	.12	.14	.16	.19	.21
180	.02	.04	.06	.08	.11	.13	.15	.17	.19
200	.02	.04	.06	.08	.09	.11	.13	.15	.17
220	.02	.03	.05	.07	.09	.10	.12	.14	.15
240	.02	.03	.05	.06	.08	.09	.11	.13	.14

Blood Alcohol Concentration for Females

Weight	Number of drinks consumed per hour								
	1	2	3	4	5	6	7	8	9
100	0.05	.09	.14	.18	.23	.27	.32	.36	.41
120	0.03	.08	.11	.15	.19	.23	.27	.30	.34
140	0.03	.07	.10	.13	.16	.19	.23	.26	.29
160	0.03	.06	.09	.11	.14	.17	.20	.23	.26
180	0.03	.05	.08	.10	.13	.15	.18	.20	.23
200	0.02	.05	.07	.09	.11	.14	.16	.18	.20
220	0.02	.04	.06	.08	.10	.12	.14	.17	.19
240	0.02	.04	.06	.08	.09	.11	.13	.15	.17

Facilitator Dialogue:

We just mentioned that your body is affected by the amount of alcohol you consume. One way to measure the amount of alcohol in your body is by looking at the amount of alcohol circulating in your blood, or BAC. We are passing around BAC cards, and I will explain to you what it means. Please take the card that corresponds with your weight. These cards are sex-specific. BAC stands for "Blood Alcohol Content." This is also known as Blood Alcohol Level.

The number represents the concentration of alcohol in your blood. For example, a BAC of .10 means that .1% of your bloodstream is made up of alcohol.

Notice these things about your personal cards:
- *At the top should be your weight and sex.*
- *Below is the number of hours spent drinking.*
- *On the left side is the number of drinks consumed.*
- *Match the number of drinks consumed with the number of hours spent drinking to find your blood alcohol content, represented by the numbers in the middle of the card.*

Understanding your BAC enables you to enjoy the things you like about drinking, drink responsibly, and prevent the not-so-good things about alcohol use from happening.

The cards provided give you an idea of what would happen if you never drank before and consumed a certain amount of alcohol (particularly as referenced in the lower BAC levels). However, you might experience the following at different BAC levels.

Notice each level and how many drinks it would take for you to get to that level by looking at your BAC card. Let's highlight a couple of BAC levels.

BAC Levels

Go through these levels quickly. If participants express surprise or shock, reflect after each level.

Facilitator Dialogue:
- *At .02, many people begin to feel relaxed.*

- *At .04, relaxation continues and a buzz develops.*

- *Up to but not exceeding .06, people may have lower inhibitions and sense warmth, feel euphoric, experience intense emotions, and behave in an exaggerated manner. Cognitive judgment is impaired. Up to but not exceeding this point is where you may feel the good things about alcohol.*

- *At .08, motor coordination is impaired, which is why this is the legal driving limit in the state of California if you are 21 years or over. If you are under 21 years, ANY alcohol use may result in a DUI. Remember that reaction times are slower even with your first drink.*

- *At .10, there is clear deterioration in cognitive judgment and motor coordination. One may experience nausea here.*

- *Between .15-.25 people may experience blackouts.*

- *From .25-.35 people may pass out, lose consciousness, and there is a risk of death.*

- *.40-.45 can be associated with a lethal dose.*

Here, pause and check in with the participants. Ask them what questions they have.

Factors that Affect BAC

Facilitator Dialogue:
What factors may affect your BAC?

Let participants respond to this question. Correct any false information and provide them with accurate information. Make sure to cover all of the following:

Facilitator Dialogue:
- *First, how much alcohol you drink affects your BAC. If you drink more, you will reach a higher BAC.*
- *Also, the strength of the drink or percentage of alcohol (a 12 oz. beer compared to a Long Island Iced Tea have very different % alcohol). If you consume 4 oz. of liquor, you will reach a higher BAC than if you consume 4 oz. of wine, or 4 oz. of beer.*

- *Food eaten along with drinking alcohol will result in a delayed BAC because the alcohol enters the bloodstream at a slower rate.*
- *Also, the type of mixer used affects your BAC. Drinking water (or alternating drinks) while consuming alcohol slows the absorption process while carbonated beverages like soda will speed it up. Carbon dioxide speeds the alcohol through the stomach and intestine into the bloodstream, creating a rapid rise in BAC. For instance, if you are drinking a rum and Coke, you will reach your BAC faster than if you were to drink only rum. The soda acts as a catalyst for the alcohol.*
- *As we mentioned earlier, women reach higher BACs faster and tend to stay intoxicated longer because of the physiological differences between men and women.*
- *Time is the only thing that can reduce your BAC—not coffee, a cold shower, or a run around the block. One thing to keep in mind is that tolerance affects how you feel but not the actual content of alcohol in the bloodstream (BAC). You still reach the same BAC if you have a higher tolerance, because tolerance only affects the way you experience alcohol, not the amount of alcohol in your blood.*

Here you may want to use the "Clone Myself" example. If I were to clone myself, and we both have six beers, I would have a higher tolerance than my clone, who is new to drinking. She may be stumbling about and slurring her words, while I stand and talk perfectly, yet our BAC levels would be the same. Why does the clone have an advantage? (The answer is because her body is giving her cues that her BAC is high, making it easier for her to know when to stop, and she doesn't have to spend as much money on alcohol.) Describe conditioning and different settings: how the body overcompensates to prepare for substances and how tolerance is like weight—you can gain or lose it.

Goal
The goal of this section is to help participants understand how alcohol is measured in their bodies so that they can monitor the amount of alcohol they consume and to provide participants with knowledge and information about BAC to help them maximize the good things about alcohol by not drinking too much. The strategies to avoid the risky effects of drinking allow participants to increase self-efficacy. While this is a purely informational section, it is necessary in building awareness of one's own drinking.

Biphasic Response of Alcohol (5 minutes)
Overview
The point of the biphasic discussion is to help students become aware of how to enjoy alcohol if a person chooses to drink, and how to avoid the negative things about alcohol. It is important to highlight that those good things diminish beyond the .05-.06 level. Also, it is important to include non-drinkers and point out that you can experience good things from a BAC of .00 to a BAC of .06.

Instructions
This is an interactive piece, so allow participants to respond.

Facilitator Dialogue:
So you are at a party...When people start to lose their "buzz," what do they usually do?
Close-ended response expected: Drink.
Do they get it back?
Close-ended response expected: No.
What does happen?
Close-ended response expected: They get drunker.

If participants say that they do get the buzz back, ask if this buzz is as good as the initial buzz. It is okay to ask students to describe what a buzz is. Chances are they are confusing the buzz with being over the limit and being drunk.

Facilitator Dialogue:
Most people are not successful in getting their buzz back after it's gone because of something called the "biphasic response" of alcohol. Most people believe in the cultural myth that the more you drink the better you feel.

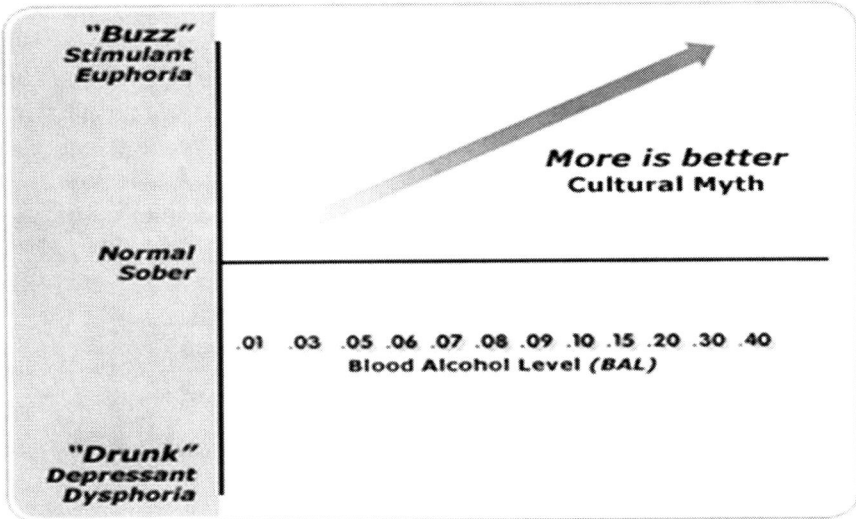

"Buzz"
Stimulant
Euphoria

More is better
Cultural Myth

Normal
Sober

.01 .03 .05 .06 .07 .08 .09 .10 .15 .20 .30 .40
Blood Alcohol Level (BAL)

"Drunk"
Depressant
Dysphoria

In reality, there is a biphasic effect. Biphasic refers to the two phases or effects of alcohol on the body.

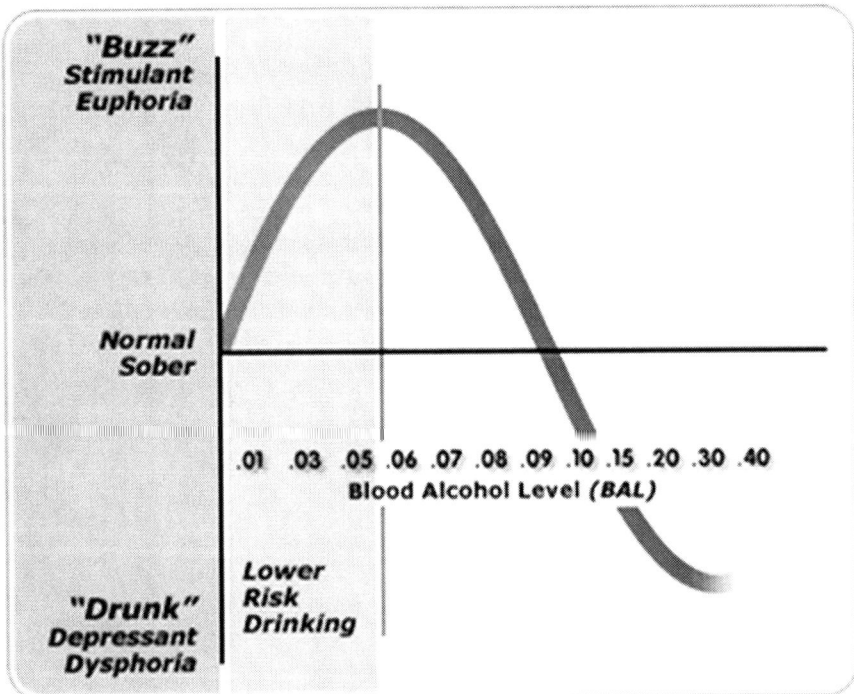

"Buzz"
Stimulant
Euphoria

Normal
Sober

.01 .03 .05 .06 .07 .08 .09 .10 .15 .20 .30 .40
Blood Alcohol Level (BAL)

Lower
Risk
Drinking

"Drunk"
Depressant
Dysphoria

Facilitator Dialogue:
The first phase consists of feeling stimulated, excited, and euphoric. The second phase consists of depressant effects, such as slowed-down body processes and depressed feelings.

The good feelings are typically associated with the rise in your BAC level. Thus, as you begin consuming alcohol, you feel good effects. However, as your BAC rises above .05-.06, you are more likely to experience the not-so-good effects of alcohol. This point is called the "point of diminishing returns," meaning that it is difficult, if not impossible, to get those good feelings or "buzz" back. If you drink too much, you are more likely to experience the depressant effects of alcohol. This is where the shift occurs and after this point, the body experiences only the depressant effects of alcohol.

Please check your BAC card for your own personal .05-.06 level. It might be helpful to think about how long a party usually lasts and look at the BAC card for the .05-.06 level and your own personal number of drinks. Once you get to a BAC of .05-.06, you will likely not experience any more intense good feelings.

On the right side of your BAC card is the description of the green, blue, and red zones. If you are going to drink, it is best to stay in your green zone (up to, but not exceeding, the .05-.06 level). The level of drinking associated with the blue and red zones is linked with increased risk levels.

Speaking of risky drinking levels, how many of you know someone who has been hospitalized because of her or his drinking?

What was this experience like for you or for them?

This question may pose some strong feelings. Be cognizant of these potential feelings and really meet the participant where she or he is at. Reflect feelings back and be empathetic.

Facilitator Dialogue:
This may happen anywhere around .20 and above.

Some of the symptoms of alcohol poisoning to look out for are hypothermia or cold, clammy skin, slowed breathing (less than nine breaths per minute), unconsciousness (without being able to be awakened), vomiting while passed out, slow pulse (50 or below and dropping), and no pain response. If you think your friend has alcohol poisoning, call x222 on campus or 911 off of campus. Also, if your friend is passed out or vomiting, lay her/him on his/her side with the arm extended beneath the head. This will help in preventing asphyxiation from vomit, which is a common cause of death in alcohol poisoning cases.

Protective Strategies

Facilitator Dialogue:
What strategies do you use for avoiding either drinking if you do not want to or drinking in excess if you are going to drink? What are some ways you can protect yourself from the riskier consequences (associated with the blue and red zones) from happening to you? What are some strategies that will help prevent the riskier consequences of drinking? Drinking slowly and moderately will increase your chances to maintain your buzz and help you avoid the not-so-good effects of alcohol.

1. Have participants discuss their own strategies to maintain the peak buzz level or lower. Refer to Martens et al. (2005) for several protective strategies.
2. Some examples of protective strategies include:
   - Setting moderate limits: Have a plan for the night as to how much you are going to drink and how you will go about executing that plan. Stick to your plan. Remember that the BAC for driving is .08 and remember the definition of "one standard drink."
   - Try to avoid drinking games and pre-partying. If you are going to engage in these activities, maintain caution and do not over-drink.
   - Remember that it takes some time for the effects of alcohol to hit you. If you drink a lot in a short period of time, you may not "feel" drunk right away.
   - Do not drink liquor (as opposed to beer) in drinking games.
   - Leave if you are not comfortable.
   - How to handle pressure from peers (if a simple "no" is not enough).
   - Most people won't notice how much you are drinking; your friends should still be able to have a good time with you even if you are not drinking as much as they are.
   - Make an excuse (test/paper/work tomorrow; driving; at your

limit; don' t want to).
- Make your own drinks, and make them less strong.
- If friends notice you "nursing a drink," tell them that you just went and filled up another one a little while ago.
3. Drinking and negative emotions
   - If you are drinking to handle school or life stressors, anxiety, or depression, seek help from friends, family members, or Student Psychological Services.
   - Think of other ways you can improve your mood.

Facilitator Dialogue:
Think about why you use drinking to improve your mood or social skills. What skills have you used in the past and what skills do you have now to help you handle anxiety or socially anxious situations without the use of alcohol?

Group Break and Questions (5 minutes)

Overview
Since the session is rather lengthy, it may be necessary to take a short break. This will help participants reflect on what they have heard and prepare them for the next discussion. This break is typically only used for the women's group sessions, as they tend to last longer than the men's group sessions.

Instructions
Tell participants that we would like to take a short break now. Point out where the bathroom is. If no one responds or gets up, ask if they would like to continue without a break.

This is the perfect opportunity to check in with everyone. Ask what questions they may have.

Facilitator Dialogue:
What questions or comments came up for you during the break?

Goal
The group break is not always necessary, but should be proposed to participants. It may be necessary to break so that participants can recharge and collect their thoughts on the process thus far.

Reasons for Drinking Discussion – Designed For Women's Groups (10-15 minutes)

Overview
The main focus of the reasons for drinking discussion is to encourage change talk and help participants to recognize why they drink. Research shows that women and men drink for very similar reasons, but there is one significant difference: women drink for relationship and bonding reasons. When speaking with women, it is important to specifically address the reasons women drink. This is a very integral part of the intervention and should be given as much time as needed. This section is typically used only in sessions with women, but may also be used with men's groups.

Instructions
Reiterate to the participants that this is a confidential project and that everything that is shared stays in the room. You want to create a comfortable, welcoming, and non-confrontational environment for the students.

Facilitator Dialogue:
If it's cool with you, let's discuss the reasons women either drink or don't drink, and the role alcohol plays in the lives of women [or men]. As we discussed before, we are looking to you for information on this topic because you are a female [or male] college student and can provide us with more specific knowledge about the reasons women [or men] at LMU, and specifically all of you, drink alcohol.

Please be as open and honest as you can. Feel free to give your opinions as often as you like. For example, you may feel similarly to what someone has expressed or you may feel differently, and both of those opinions are important to us.

Use as few closed-ended questions as possible, use a few open-ended questions, and mostly reflect back what participants say in a manner that prompts further discussion of the topic they are describing.

Facilitator Dialogue:
What are the reasons that women [or men] drink? What are the reasons women [or men] don't drink? What about you specifically?

Information regarding the consequences of alcohol use can be assimilated into this discussion. However, the discussion should be generated by the group participants. End with a double-sided summary/reflection, where you summarize the reasons women (or men) drink and the reasons women don't drink. Make sure that the role of alcohol in relationships is always discussed. If this is not brought up naturally in the group, then ask directly, "How does alcohol affect your relationships?"

Goal
The goal of this section is to help participants understand more fully the reasons women (or men) drink in general and their own personal reasons for drinking. Often, individuals are not very aware of why they drink; knowing and understanding this can help them address any changes necessary while providing motivation for change.

Decisional Balance with Open-Ended Discussion (15 Minutes)

Overview
The decisional balance takes the "Reasons for Drinking Discussion" a step further and helps participants to recognize reasons why they drink and reasons why they don't drink. It aids individuals in recognizing their ambivalence to change, examining personal discrepancies between goals and behavior, and clarifying their motivating factors for change. Individually, participants generate a list of reasons for not drinking less (if a drinker), or reasons for not staying a non-drinker (if a non-drinker). Then they list reasons for drinking less than they presently do (if a drinker) or reasons for staying a non-drinker (if a non-drinker). They rate the reasons to further recognize the importance of their drinking. If the "Reasons for Drinking Discussion" is not conducted as a group exercise, have the participants generate a list of reasons for (pros) and reasons against (cons) drinking less than they presently do.

Instructions
Guide participants to construct a decisional balance regarding their reasons for (pros) and reasons against (cons) changing their drinking. It is important that the students know that "changing drinking" does not necessarily mean abstinence. They can interpret change as whatever is important for them. It is important to be clear in this section, as students are often confused by the wording. However, this section is worded specifically to help students think more about why they are not drinking less. Be patient with the participants. You may have to repeat yourself.

Facilitator Dialogue:
Thank you all for being so open and sharing with us your reasons for drinking and not drinking. Next, if it's cool with all of you, we would like you to record your own personal reasons why you might choose to drink less or maintain your non-drinking behavior.

Please take a look at this worksheet. For those of you who consider yourselves drinkers, up on the top left side of the sheet write "Not drinking less than I do now" and go ahead and list your own personal reasons for not drinking less, basically why would you want to continue drinking, and what your reasons are for drinking. For those of you who consider yourselves non-drinkers, please write "Not staying a non-drinker" and list your personal reasons why you may want to begin drinking or any obstacles you may run into that may make you think about drinking. You do not have to list ten reasons, just as many as are personal and relevant for you. You may want to think about what we have covered today, especially in the discussion we just had.

Some sample reasons for not drinking less or not staying a non-drinker are:
- *Drinking helps me keep my mind off my problems.*
- *Drinking helps me have fun with my friends.*
- *People seem to like me better when I am drinking.*
- *Drinking helps give me energy and keeps me going.*
- *Drinking makes me more relaxed and less tense.*
- *Drinking gives me more courage.*
- *I find it easier to express my feelings when I drink.*

Now please go through and rate each reason independently by writing a number between "0" and "10" next to each reason. A "0" rating would not be an important reason to you. A "10" rating would be a highly important reason to you. Keep in mind that you can have more than one item rated at the same number; this is a rating, not a ranking.

Okay. Now we are going to go on to the next side of the sheet. On the right side, if you consider yourself a drinker, go ahead and write, "Drinking less than I do now" and list any personal reasons you may have for reducing your drinking. And if you consider yourself a non-drinker, go ahead and write "Staying a non-drinker" and write your own personal reasons for staying a non-drinker. Why would you not want to begin drinking? Again, you don't have to write 10 reasons, just as many as are important to you.

Some sample reasons for drinking less or staying a non-drinker are:

- *I do not like myself when I drink.*
- *Drinking causes problems with others (romantic relationships, friends).*
- *I am setting a bad example for others when I drink.*
- *I would have more money to spend on other things.*
- *My drinking makes me feel out of control.*
- *Drinking can negatively influence schoolwork performance and damage my grades.*
- *After drinking, I often wake up feeling down (hangovers or depression).*
- *Drinking could land me in trouble with the law.*
- *Drinking gets in the way of other things I want to do.*

Now please go through again and rate each reason on the right side from "0" to "10" just as you did on the left side. Keep in mind that you can have more than one item rated at the same number; this is a rating, not a ranking.

Draw the following ruler for participants to use as a scale.
0----1-----2---3----4----5----6-----7-----8----9----10
Not important   Moderately   Extremely

Once you have completed that, give each list an overall rating from "0" to "10." In other words, give each side—all of your reasons on the left together and all of your reasons on the right together—a rating from "0" to "10" indicating how important each side is to you.

Finally, ask participants to share the reason they rated the highest and why it is most important to them. Reaffirm and reflect what participants say as their most important reason. Ask them why it is important to them (even if it seems obvious) and support their reasons with reflective listening. Summarize all responses after all participants have responded. This is typically done only in the men's sessions, but may be done in women's groups as well.

Facilitator Dialogue:
We've talked a lot about drinking and drinking less. If you were going to make a change, what would you do? How would you do it?

This last question leads into the next piece, where participants set a goal for themselves.

Goal
The goal of the decisional balance is to help participants weigh the costs and benefits of reducing their drinking in some form. It is an essential part of Motivational Interviewing and helps participants personally confront what is more important to them, for example, continuing to drink at the same level or achieving their long- and short-term goals.

Decisional Balance Worksheet
ID Number: _____

- -- --- --- -- -- -- -- --- --- -- -- -- --	- -- -- -- -- --- --- -- -- -- -- --- ---

Making Motivational Statement/Setting a Behavioral Goal
(5 Minutes)

Overview
Each student sets and shares with the group a behavioral goal for how he or she will drink in the next 30 days. This activity helps students to personalize the message of the group session and leads the participants to change, if they need to and/or are ready to.

Instructions
First, participants assess where they are at in terms of changing their drinking behavior and then they set their goals.

Facilitator Dialogue:
Now, if it makes sense, we are going to fill out another sheet. The first question asks you about your readiness to change your drinking—if you've ever thought about it or if you have changed your behavior already. Please circle the number that corresponds to where you are currently in terms of your change.

Next, we would like to set a personal behavioral goal. What could you do if you wanted to drink less? Please think of a motivational goal for how you will drink in the next 30 days. It may be something as simple as, "I will drink less than I do now," or "I will drink only two times per week," or "I will continue to not drink." This goal can be anything related to your drinking. However you choose to drink is a personal decision. Be aware of how you choose to drink and the reasons why you choose to drink. Write your goal down on the form and the card provided. The card is for you to keep.

Give participants ideas about what their goals may be.

Please complete the rest of the sheet. When you are done, please write your ID number on top, turn them over, and pass them in.

Remember, the important message from today's group is to be mindful of your decisions.

Now let's share our behavioral goals. What are some barriers that we may experience in attempting to achieve these goals? What are your strategies for handling these challenges and difficulties?

Ask participants to share their goals with the group. Tell participants that if for personal reasons they do not wish to share their specific goals, to please state whether their goal is a reduction or maintenance of current behavior.

Often by this point participants are tired, so be patient. Give them time to talk. Also, if no one is talking it may be helpful to ask, "How about hearing from someone we haven't heard from?" Again, tell participants that if for personal reasons they do not wish to share their specific goals, to please state whether their goal is a reduction or maintenance of behavior.

Goal
Making motivational goals and having them supported by the group will help participants in reducing their drinking and help make their decisions concrete.

Assessment of Drinking Worksheet

ID Number _____

On the ruler below, please circle the number that best describes how you feel *RIGHT NOW about your drinking*:

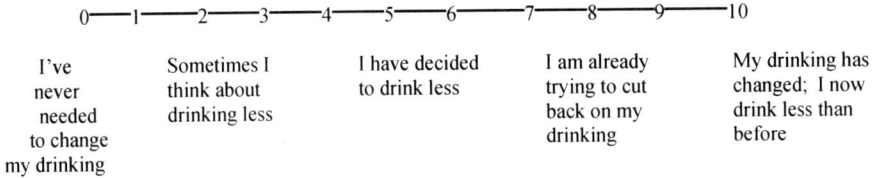

0——1————2————3————4————5————6————7————8————9————10

| I've never needed to change my drinking | Sometimes I think about drinking less | I have decided to drink less | I am already trying to cut back on my drinking | My drinking has changed; I now drink less than before |

On the lines below, write down a behavioral goal that describes how you will drink in the next 30 days:

_____

_____

_____

_____

How does this goal relate to your own drinking behavior prior to today's group?

This goal represents (check one)

_____ a reduction in behavior

_____ a maintenance of behavior

_____ an increase in behavior

At this moment, how important is it that you achieve your goal?

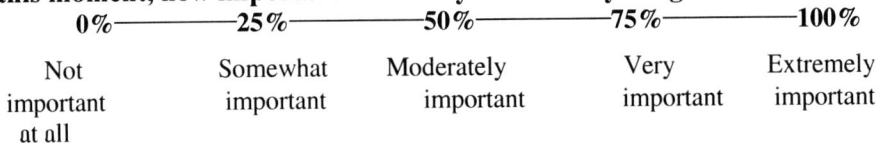

0%————25%————50%————75%————100%

| Not important at all | Somewhat important | Moderately important | Very important | Extremely important |

The importance of my goal is _____%

How confident are you that you will achieve your goal?

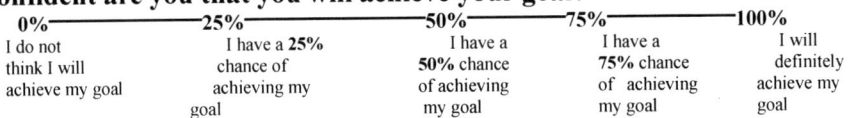

0%————25%————50%————75%————100%

| I do not think I will achieve my goal | I have a 25% chance of achieving my goal | I have a 50% chance of achieving my goal | I have a 75% chance of achieving my goal | I will definitely achieve my goal |

I am _____% confident that I will achieve my goal.

The following items ask about your intended behavior in the _NEXT WEEK (7 days)_:
How many **days** *in the next week* do you intend to drink? _____
How many **drinks** do you intend to have, **per drinking occasion**, *in the next week?* _____
What is the **maximum** number of drinks you intend to drink **on one occasion** *in the next week?*_____

Drinking Diary Follow-Up (5 Minutes)
Overview
Here we explain how diaries will be completed for the next ten weeks (if volunteer participant) or the next twelve weeks (if judicial participant).

Diary follow-up will be different depending on how your institution decides to collect them. Please see Chapter VIII of this manual for different collection methods and inform participants of their part in the process accordingly. Be sure to fully explain the diaries and how they are to be completed. Remind them of the sensitive nature of the diary and assure them of confidentiality.

Participant Feedback (5 Minutes)
Overview
Participants indicate what they liked best and what they liked least about the group. This is helpful for Heads UP personnel to make improvements and also to evaluate how sessions are going.

Instructions
Finally, we'd like to ask you to please complete the Participant Feedback sheet, which asks you what was helpful and not helpful about the session. This information is very helpful for us to improve the project in the future.

We have compiled a brochure about the consequences of alcohol as well as references from where to obtain additional information, if you are interested in learning more about the topics. Once you are finished, please come up to one of us, and we will give you your brochure and your check [if he or she is a volunteer participant].

We thank you for your participation!

Goal
The goal of the end of group questionnaire is to qualitatively assess the group and determine if intended drinking changed immediately after the intervention. The diaries serve as a post-intervention follow-up assessment and aid the intervention by having participants monitor their drinking over the course of ten or twelve weeks.

This concludes the session!

Participant Feedback Worksheet
ID Number:_____

1.   What was helpful about this group?

_____
_____
_____
_____

What was not helpful about this group?

_____
_____
_____
_____

What is your overall response to this group?

_____
_____
_____
_____

2.   Please rate your level of disclosure, or how much you shared about yourself during this group.
     Please mark an X below.
     0------------1--------------2-------------3--------------4
     Almost Nothing   A Great Deal
3.   Please rate the group level of disclosure, or how much you think the group as a whole shared with each other. Please mark an X below.

     0------------1--------------2------------3-------------4
     Almost Nothing   A Great Deal
4.   Please rate how helpful you think this group was. Please mark an X below.

     0----1-----2-----3-----4-----5----6---7----8----9--10
     Not At All Helpful   Moderately Helpful   Extremely Helpful

5.   Are you currently involved in therapy or another type of intervention?
     ____ YES   ____NO

6.   If so, is this related to alcohol issues?
     _____
     _____

Chapter VIII

Post-Group Procedures

Once you have completed the intervention group, post-group procedures begin. An integral part of the Heads UP intervention program is the ten or twelve-week diary follow-up process. Post-group data collection will vary depending on how participants are recruited to participate. Those referred by judicial affairs will complete diaries for twelve weeks (three months) to complete a current sanction and avoid further sanction, whereas volunteer participants will complete diaries for ten weeks and may be rewarded for diary completion with incentives (see examples below). It is important to use incentives specific to your population.

The following procedures are meant to be conducted in concert with your judicial affairs department.

What Does the Diary Collection Include?
Diary collection consists of either a weekly or monthly calendar, in which participants are asked to report the number of standard alcoholic drinks they had on each and every day, as well as intended drinking behavior for the next week. In addition, you may want to include other assessment measures (such as those listed in Chapter VI) in order to assess progress and efficacy of the intervention over time. Heads UP typically uses the Ready to Change Ruler (LaBrie, J. W., Quinlan, T., Schiffman, J., & Earleywine, M. (2005) and the Duke Health Profile (Parkerson, G. R. Jr., Broadhead, W. E., & Tse, C. K. (1990). A sample of both the weekly and monthly diary calendar is included at the end of this section.

Process of Diary Collection
In establishing the Heads UP program at your institution, it is important to clearly designate how participants will return the diary information to you for data analysis and to ensure the highest retention rates and that judicial requirements are met. It is important to assess your institution's needs regarding data collection and management and, in turn, the best data collection procedure for your institution. The following are four ways in which participants may submit their diaries: in person, via campus mail, via email, and via an online data management system.

Diary Collection Methods
Depending on your staff and funding, diaries can be distributed and received in the following ways:

In-person Diary Collection

In-person diary collection is the simplest, but may be the most time consuming. For this type of collection, a paper diary is used. Either weekly or monthly, each participant is asked to come to the research office location and pick up a diary and drop off a completed diary for the previous week or month. The Heads UP staff member should enter the date on Day 1 and the date on Day 7 or 30 of the calendar, so the participant has either a seven or 30-day window to record responses, and will have the date when the diary needs to be returned.

When doing the in-person diary collection, it may be best to do the monthly diary, as it may be time-consuming and potentially overwhelming to have participants at your office weekly. However, there are foreseeable risks in choosing the paper in-person diary collection method. First, since participants take the diary home with them, they may not complete it on a daily basis and may wait until the day before it is due to complete it, thus relying on memory, which is especially difficult when using the monthly diary. Second, many students may not get the diary back on time, and therefore may not begin the next diary on time. If this method is chosen, reminder emails should be sent to each participant reminding them of the date they should come in to complete their diary. This method may be considered the least reliable.

Campus Mail Diary Collection

Participants can be mailed a paper copy of the diary and follow-up questions either monthly or weekly. They can then either hand-deliver the completed diary to the Heads UP office or mail the diary back to the office. These options should be explicitly stated for participants so they can return the questionnaires in a timely fashion.

Email Diary Collection

Email is a more efficient way of collecting diaries, as you can send a mass email through Microsoft Word's mail merge application or from your own email address. If you choose this method, it may be helpful to set up an email address specifically for Heads UP, to which students may send their completed diaries. Simply attach the Word document diary form to the email and send it out. Participants can then download the diary from the email, save it to their computer, update it daily with the number of drinks they consumed, and complete the other assessments prior to emailing the diary back. Another option is entering the entire diary into the body of the text so that the participant can simply reply to the email and fill out their responses in the reply. This may not be the best method if diaries are monthly, since participants would have to update their response email for 30 days. Depending upon your choice of monthly or weekly diaries, the participants should return the diaries via email accordingly.

Online Diary Collection
An online management and dissemination system may be purchased (such as DatStat Illume; http://datstatillume.com/) or set up through a free-online system (such as Survey Monkey; http:// surveymonkey.com/). These systems allow you to create surveys, automate when surveys are sent out, and allow participants to complete surveys by clicking a link to the survey and completing it online. By doing so, participants never have to submit the survey in person, and results are automatically submitted once they finish answering the questions online. Protocol for online systems will vary depending on the survey system used.

In recent years, Heads UP at Loyola Marymount University has employed DatStat Illume, an online survey design, management, and collection system. Students, clinicians, researchers, and school personnel may all prefer to use electronic means of data collection and analysis in order to decrease data entry errors and improve efficacy and efficiency. If the data collection is completed electronically, more time is allowed during the group intervention for discussion rather than data collection. By implementing DatStat Illume or other similar systems your program will be able to receive feedback from your participants in a timely and well-organized manner. Additionally, online systems ensure exceptionally high retention rates; at Loyola Marymount University, we have retention rates of 95-99% depending on the population, which is unheard of in the field of self-report research. The protocol ensures the anonymity of each participant with 128-bit encryption. However, if you are interested in tracking changes for each individual participant, you may establish your data collection to evaluate individual level progress.

Monitoring Diaries
Depending on the type of system you choose to collect diaries, monitoring diary completion will vary. It is recommended that a Microsoft Excel spreadsheet be set up to contain the participant number and space for each diary. Once each diary is complete, you can indicate that the participant has completed the diary by putting a "1" or "x" in the space for that diary and participant. This will help you see quickly who has and has not completed the diary for that week (or month).

It is important to monitor diaries so that they are completed in a timely fashion. Email or call participants who have not completed their diaries the day following the due date of the diary. If you use an email or online system, include the diary (or link to the diary) in the email so participants can easily complete it.

Incentives
In order to maximize the number of participants who complete each diary, some programs may choose to offer incentives for volunteer participants upon the completion of diary-keeping. Incentives should be distributed as soon as diaries are completed. For in-person diary completion, incentives should be given out immediately after participants hand in the diary. For all other participants, incentives may be mailed to campus mailboxes or be held at the Heads UP research office for pick-up. If you choose to hold incentives at the office for pick-up, notify participants who have completed the diary that their incentive is at the office. Incentives may include coupons for pizza, cash, Heads UP promotional items (which may include water bottles, t-shirts, Frisbees, or other items students may be interested in) and gift cards. Incentives are dependent upon funds for the program or may not be appropriate to offer.

Diary Notification Procedures
In addition to the process of diary collection via personal collection, notification procedures have been established in order to uniformly contact participants regarding their data. The following are the Heads UP procedures to notify participants of the due dates for their drinking diaries.

Judicial Participants:
Email participants two to three days prior to due date.
- Use letter template.
- Use Heads UP email account for all contact with participants.
- Utilize appropriate distribution list when emailing participants.
- Send "carbon copy" (cc) to Heads UP Email account.
- Place participant addresses in the blind carbon copy (bcc) location so they cannot see each other's email addresses.
- Call and email participants on diary due date.
- Remind participants of the date their diary is due.
- Inform participants that they have to return their diary as soon as possible. If the diary is not returned by the due date, they may be fined by Judicial Affairs.
- Indicate where and when participants may return their diaries.

- On each day the diary is late, follow up with an email and phone call for ten days following due date.
- Even after the diary is due, call the participants and tell them that their diary needs to be turned in. If the diary is not received within the next day or two, refer them to Judicial Affairs.
- Stop making contact after the ten-day grace period.

If the participant fails to return the diary within the requisite ten days:
- Notify Judicial Affairs of the participant's non-compliance.
- On the participant Excel spreadsheet, highlight the participant's row in red to indicate he or she has been dropped from the program.
- If the Heads UP program is being utilized through your judicial department, establish a consistent check-in time with Judicial Affairs personnel to review and update information regarding participant attendance. It may be best to set up correspondence with the Judicial Affairs office and communicate the participant's completion through email.

Volunteer Participants:
Email participants three days prior to due date.
- Use letter template.
- Use Heads UP email account for all contact with participants.
- Utilize appropriate distribution list when emailing participants.
- cc to Heads UP email account.
- Place email addresses in the bcc so participants cannot view the list of participants.
- Call and email participants the day the diary is due.
- Remind participants of the diary due date.
- Tell them their data is very important to the integrity of the project and remind them that all of their information is completely confidential.
- Tell them that if they return the diaries they will receive an incentive.
- Indicate where and when they can return their diaries.
- For up to ten days after the due date, follow up daily with an email or phone call.

WEEKLY BEHAVIORAL DIARY

ID Number: _____

The following pages contain a diary for you to keep track of your drinking behavior over the next 30 days. Please try to fill in each event as soon as possible after it occurs. Additional questions are at the end of the diary. Answer these questions prior to submitting your diary. Your honesty is essential for the success of this study. These responses are strictly confidential and are used for research purposes only. Your name will never be attached to them. To protect your own confidentiality, please keep this diary in a location where you alone have access to it and return it immediately upon completion.

How many drinks did you have on each of the following days?

Monday - Date	_____ drinks
Tuesday - Date	_____ drinks
Wednesday - Date	_____ drinks
Thursday - Date	_____ drinks
Friday - Date	_____ drinks
Saturday - Date	_____ drinks
Sunday - Date	_____ drinks

The following items ask about your intended behavior in the NEXT WEEK (7 days).

On how many days do you intend to drink during the next week?
_____ days

How many drinks do you intend to drink on average in the next week?
_____ drinks

What is the maximum number of drinks you intend to drink at one time in the next week?
_____ drinks

On the ruler below, please rate how RELAXED or TENSE you have been (DURING THE PAST WEEK):

0—1—2—3—4—5—6—7—8—9—10
Very Tense   Not Tense At All

On the ruler below, please choose the number that best describes how you feel RIGHT NOW:

0—1—2—3—4—5—6—7—8—9—10

I've never needed to change my drinking	Sometimes I think about drinking less	I have decided to drink less	I am already trying to cut back on my drinking	My drinking has changed; I now drink less than before

MONTHLY BEHAVIORAL DIARY
ID Number: _____

The following pages contain a diary for you to keep track of your drinking behavior over the next 30 days. Please try to fill in each event as soon as possible after it occurs. Additional questions are at the end of the diary. Answer these questions prior to submitting your diary. Your honesty is essential for the success of this study. These responses are strictly confidential and are used for research purposes only. Your name will never be attached to them. To protect your own confidentiality, please keep this diary in a location where you alone have access to it and return it immediately upon completion.

Day/ Date	Total # drinks per day	Day/ Date	Total # drinks per day
Day 1/		Day 16/	
Day 2/		Day 17/	
Day 3/		Day 18/	
Day 4/		Day 19/	
Day 5/		Day 20/	
Day 6/		Day 21/	
Day 7/		Day 22/	
Day 8/		Day 23/	
Day 9/		Day 24/	
Day 10/		Day 25/	
Day 11/		Day 26/	
Day 12/		Day 27/	
Day 13/		Day 28/	
Day 14/		Day 29/	
Day 15/		Day 30/	

The following items ask about your intended behavior in the
NEXT MONTH (30 days).

On how many days per week do you intend to drink?
_____ days

On how many days do you intend to drink in the next 30 days?
_____ days

On average, how many drinks do you intend to drink when you do drink?
_____ drinks

During the next 30 days, what is the maximum number of drinks you intend
to drink <u>on one occasion</u>?
_____ drinks

On the ruler below, please choose the number that
best describes how you feel RIGHT NOW:

0——1——2——3——4——5——6——7——8——9——10

I've never needed to change my drinking	Sometimes I think about drinking less	I have decided to drink less	I am already trying to cut back on my drinking	My drinking has changed; I now drink less than before

Chapter IX

Conclusion and Future Directions

Implementation at Your Institution

While Heads UP is a manualized prevention/treatment program, it is flexible and can be tailored to fit the needs of your school. At the heart of the Heads UP intervention program is the integration of Motivational Interviewing and the brief group setting. Utilizing the techniques of MI into your program and implementing the program to groups, rather than individuals, will improve efficacy and the reach of your program, with the hope of motivating change and reduced problematic drinking in a wider population. Our hope is that Heads UP will have the same culture-changing effect at your institution that it has had at Loyola Marymount University.

Future Directions

Due to the success of Heads UP as a first-line intervention for alcohol policy violations on campus, Heads UP has created a second-line intervention for repeat alcohol policy violations. This second-line intervention is an individual adaptation of BASICS (Brief Alcohol Screening and Intervention for College Students; Dimeff, Baer, Kivlahan, and Marlatt) and Motivational Interviewing (Miller & Rollnick). Currently, this new intervention is being tested and assessed at Loyola Marymount University.

Appendix A
Heads UP Men Intervention Script
Introduction and Review of Consent

Facilitator Dialogue:
You have been sanctioned by the Office of Judicial Affairs to receive Heads UP, so I would like to tell you a bit about the program. First, I would like to introduce myself [and co-facilitators].

Tell participants your name and position at Heads UP and allow co-facilitators (if any) to introduce themselves.

Facilitator Dialogue:
Heads UP is a research project based in the Psychology Department. It is under the direction of Dr. Joseph LaBrie. Many of you probably know him or at least remember him talking at your orientation. Heads UP is completely separate from Judicial Affairs. Our relationship with them is that we provide a service to them by running groups with you guys and they provide us with participants for our research study. We only collect your names so that we can tell Judicial Affairs who has completed the program. With that said, please know that anything we discuss in these groups will never be shared with Judicial Affairs, your RD, RAs, or anyone outside of this group. We ask you all to keep what is said in here confidential as well.

In order to take the initial questionnaire, you had to read and consent to the terms of this project. To review, the form told you that we will not share any of your information with anyone. You will use the sequence number we have provided on all the forms you fill out today and on all follow-up materials. You will <u>only</u> be identified by this sequence number. Your name will not be connected to your data in any way. We only need to use your name to inform Judicial Affairs that you have completed each part of the project. We will keep all of your answers to the questionnaires confidential, as well as anything you choose to share with the group today. Remember that all information will be kept confidential; we're only interested in the group as a whole, not individual people.

We are not here to tell you guys to never drink or that drinking is bad. Our project focuses on promoting a healthy lifestyle for all students at LMU. We are not an abstinence-only program, but more of what we call a "responsible-drinking project." If you choose to drink, we promote doing so in a responsible manner in which you do not harm yourself or others. The majority of you in here are probably under 21. While our program does not support underage drinking, please know that discussing your alcohol use in this group will never get you in trouble with your RAs or Judicial Affairs. Please feel free to share as much as you like with the group and know you will never be judged or get in trouble for admitting to alcohol use.

Timeline-Followback Calendaring of Drinking Behavior

Facilitator Dialogue:
We're going to start today with an activity by calendaring the drinking and the non-drinking you've done over the past three months. Together, we are going to come up with how much alcohol you consumed on each day during the past three months. At first this may seem difficult, but if you use a calendar like this one [show the sample calendar], *you will be surprised at how well you can remember your drinking days and patterns. A calendar is very useful in helping people recall their drinking.*

Hand out the three-month TLFB with marker dates, holidays, and campus events. Encourage students to complete TLFB independently. Although students will share events together out loud, calendaring of drinking should be done independently. Facilitators might want to consider separating friends or rearranging the seating order so that students are not tempted to work together during the TLFB.

Facilitator Dialogue:
Now let's begin. Let's start with yesterday and go back about three months. Please circle yesterday and go back three months from yesterday and circle that day [announce the date aloud]. *Cross off the days from today on and the days before three months ago* [show participants how to do this by using the sample calendar].

As you can see, standard holidays and campus events are already marked for you on the calendar to help you recall your activities around these times. What are some other significant dates that have occurred in the past three months? What are some other big on-campus events that you can remember?

Now, you come up with any other special events or holidays that have occurred in the past three months that would help your memory. These can be good things that have happened to you or not-so-good things that have happened to you: birthdays, celebrations, hospitalizations, check receipt days, and so on. They can be related to drinking or they can just be other memorable days that have occurred in the past month. We will call these "Marker Days." Fill out your own marker days on your calendars. You can use any marks you want to indicate your marker days; it is irrelevant for us to know what they are. They are simply going to be used to help you remember your drinking and non-drinking.

The idea here is to record the number of drinks you consumed each day. You will go back through each day of the calendar and write the number of standard drinks you consumed on each day. If you had no drinks on a day, mark a zero on the day.

It is important to record your drinking on the calendar in terms of standard drinks. What makes up one standard drink?

One standard drink is equal to one 12 oz. regular beer (a can or a bottle), one 4 oz. glass of wine, one 1.25 oz. shot of hard alcohol (like vodka or whiskey), one mixed drink with one 1.25 oz. shot of hard alcohol, a 10 oz. wine cooler, or an 8 oz. malt liquor.

What kinds of drinks do you normally have? How many standard drinks are included? For example, if you had a 40 oz. bottle of malt liquor, you would indicate that you drank about 5 standard drinks (malt liquor is higher in alcohol content than regular beer). Likewise, if you drank a Long Island Iced Tea with 4 shots of liquor in it, you would have had 4 standard drinks. A 12 oz. can of beer would be one standard drink. For instance, you may be holding one glass of a Long Island Iced Tea, but you are actually consuming 4 standard drinks in that one glass. What questions do you have about standard drinks?

Now, we are going to go back through the calendar every day for the past three months and mark what days you drank and how much you drank. Keep in mind this does not have to be perfect. We want you to be as accurate as possible, but we realize that it is hard for anyone to recall things perfectly. So if you can't recall, for example, whether you drank on a Monday or a Thursday of a certain week, just give it your best guess.

This goes the same for quantity of drinks—just give it your best guess. If you remember having somewhere between eight to ten drinks on a day, pick nine. If you had three to five drinks, pick four. If you didn't drink at all, mark a zero on that day. What questions do you have?

For now, we are going to start with today and go back through each day of the last two weeks together. You will write the number of drinks you drank on each day that you drank.

Start with today and take the participants back through each day of the calendar for two weeks. Then allow them to fill out the calendar on their own.

Facilitator Dialogue:
We will walk around and help you while filling these out. Remember, this doesn't need to be perfect but please try and be as accurate and honest as possible. Make sure to put down a single number for the amount of drinks, not a range. If you can't remember, just use your best guess.

Then if it makes sense, you can continue to fill out the rest of the three months on your own.

If participants are having trouble remembering drinking days, prompt them with: What activities do you participate in when you typically drink? Do you drink only on certain nights? Or is there a night when you usually always drink? While watching a television show? On a trip? If they say "a lot," ask them what they mean, and to tell you more.

Facilitator Dialogue:
When all participants are finished: *Starting with yesterday, we want you to go back over the past month and indicate on which drinking days you believe you drank five drinks in a two-hour period. Indicate those days by circling the day. Also, write an "M" on the day you drank the most in the past month. If it seems reasonable, we can talk about this later on today.*

If participant questions the five drinks in two-hour period, follow with "if you had five drinks in one setting, generally two to three hours." If there are further questions, instruct participant to use their best guess.

Encouragement and reassurance that the task is possible, is essential.

Introductions
The first facilitator begins, and then introductions are opened up to participants, and the second facilitator ends. If you feel the group is tired or particularly quiet, ask them how they feel about being in the session.

Facilitator Dialogue:
For judicial participants: *Let's now take a moment to introduce ourselves to each other. Please state your first name, your year, where you live, how you ended up here (in Heads UP), and how you feel about being here.*

For volunteer participants: *Let's now take a moment to introduce ourselves to each other. Please state your first name, where you live, and where you're from.*

Normative Data Feedback

Now I would like for us to take a look on what you guys think drinking is like here at LMU. I will ask you some questions and I want you to guess at what the answers are. All the responses I give you are based on the 2005 CORE survey given to all the students here at LMU (males, females, freshmen, sophomores, juniors, and seniors; about 1,300 students (which is about ¼ of the school), 25% from each class year). We have done similar surveys with freshmen students only, members of Greek and service organizations, and athletes and have found similar results each time. We are quite confident that we have an accurate account of drinking on campus.

Please flip one of sheets you have over and write down the numbers one through five. I am going to ask you a series of five questions and please do your best to estimate what you think the correct statistic is. Write your answer down on the sheet.

1. First what percentage of male LMU students do you think drink three or more times per week?
   - *19% (This means that 81% of male LMU students drink less than 3 times every week).*

2. What percentage of male LMU students report drinking less than five drinks during a typical drinking occasion? (They were asked, "How much do you typically drink when you do drink?")
   - *54% of males drank four or less drinks on average when drinking.*
     - *Actually, only 13% of male students reported drinking more than eight drinks during a typical drinking occasion.*

3. What percentage of male LMU students drank 10 or less drinks over the course of a typical week?
   - *77% of male students drank 10 or less drinks over the course of a typical week at school.*
     - *Actually, only 12% of male students drank 20 or more drinks over a typical week.*

What percentage of male LMU students report drinking six times per year or less?

- *25% of LMU male students reported drinking six times a year or less.*
  - o *Actually, 14% of LMU males reported not drinking at all in the past year.*

5. What percentage of male LMU students got written up and sanctioned by Judicial Affairs in the past year?
- *10% of male LMU students.*

This is just an interesting bit of information.
- *Male students who averaged five or more drinks per occasion were three times more likely to get written up than male students who drank less than five drinks per occasion.*

6. What percentage of the time is alcohol involved in the following experiences here at LMU? Students reported on the questionnaire that they experienced some sort of incident and then were asked if alcohol was involved when they experienced each incident. So, this is the percentage of the time that these incidences were reported that alcohol was involved. These stats are for all students, including women, and are important for you guys to be aware of.
- *Forced/unwanted sexual touching (i.e., being groped)   (64%)*
- *Regretted sexual intercourse   (76%)*
- *Unwanted sexual intercourse (i.e., rape) (80%)*

Decisional Balance with Open-ended Discussion

Take out the worksheet entitled "Decisional Balance." On the top somewhere, please write "Changing my drinking." Now on the left column, please write "Reasons against change" and on the right, please write "Reasons for change." We are going to make a list of all the reasons for and against changing your drinking. Take "changing your drinking" to mean "drinking less than you do now." You can consider changing your drinking to mean anything you want. It can be to reduce one night per weekend so that you only drink on Fridays and not Saturdays. It can be to reduce drinking by one or two drinks per occasion. Whatever you want it to mean.

First, think of some reasons why people would not want to change their drinking. Basically, why would anyone want to continue drinking at the level at which they currently drink?

Some sample reasons for not drinking less or not staying a non-drinker are:

- *Drinking helps me keep my mind off my problems.*
- *Drinking helps me have fun with my friends.*
- *People seem to like me better when I am drinking.*
- *Drinking helps give me energy and keeps me going.*
- *Drinking makes me more relaxed and less tense.*
- *Drinking gives me more courage.*
- *I find it easier to express my feelings when I drink.*

Write down the reasons against changing drinking that personally resonate with you. [Pause]. Once you are done, go through and rate each reason, independently from the others, on a scale between zero and 10. A zero rating means "this reason is not very important to me" and a ten rating would mean "this reason is extremely important to me." Now, rate that list as a whole based on how important all those reasons are to you when considered together.

Now we are going to generate some reasons for changing your drinking. First, why would anyone want to change their drinking to drink less than they do now?

Sample reasons for drinking less or staying a non-drinker are:

- *I do not like myself when I drink.*
- *Drinking causes problems with others (romantic relationships, friends).*
- *I am setting a bad example for others when I drink.*
- *I would have more money to spend on other things.*
- *My drinking makes me feel out of control.*
- *Drinking can negatively influence schoolwork performance and damage my grades.*
- *After drinking, I often wake up feeling down (hangovers or depression).*
- *Drinking could land me in trouble with the law.*
- *Drinking gets in the ways of other things I want to do.*

Write down the reasons for change that personally resonate with you. Now go through and rate these reasons the same way we did with the reasons against change. Give each reason a number of importance from zero to ten.

Once you complete that, give each list an overall score as a group from zero to ten.

Draw the following ruler for participants to use as a scale.
0---1----2---3----4----5-----6-----7-----8----9-----10
Not important   Moderately   Extremely

Now pick the reason for change that you rated the highest—so maybe an eight, nine, or ten. Let's go around the room and tell us what the reason was and why it was important to you. It's important to share why that reason is important to you even if it seems obvious.

We do this exercise so that you can see what is important to you personally and how reducing drinking even by just a little may help you better achieve what you want to do.

Blood Alcohol Content (BAC) Discussion

I am going to give you all a BAC card and I will explain to you what it means. BAC stands for "Blood Alcohol Content." This is also known as Blood Alcohol Level.

The number represents the concentration of alcohol in your blood. A BAC of .10 means that .1% of your bloodstream is made up of alcohol.

Notice these things about your personal cards [show participants on a sample BAC card how to use it]:
On the top should be your weight and sex. Below is the number of hours spent drinking.
On the left side is the number of drinks consumed.
Match up the number of drinks consumed with the number of hours spent drinking to find your blood alcohol content. These are the numbers in the middle of the card.
On the right side is the description of the green, blue, and red zones. If you are going to drink, it is best to stay in your green zone. The level of drinking associated with the blue and red zones is linked with increased risk levels.

Understanding your BAC could enable you to enjoy the things you like about drinking, drink responsibly, and prevent the not-so-good things about alcohol use from happening.

Notice each level and how many drinks it would take for you to get to that level by looking at your BAC card.

Let's highlight a couple of BAC levels.

- *(Up to but not exceeding) the .04-.06% level, relaxation and a buzz develops. Cognitive judgment is impaired. People may have lower inhibitions, have a sensation of warmth, feel euphoric, emotions may be intensified, and behavior may become exaggerated. Please look at your card to determine your personal level. As your BAC rises above .05-.06, you are more likely to experience the not-so-good effects of alcohol.*
- *At .08% nausea can appear, and motor coordination is impaired.*
- *Between .15-.25% people may experience blackouts.*
- *From .25%-.35% people may pass out, lose consciousness, and there is the risk of death.*
- *.40%-.45% is a lethal dose.*

What factors may affect your BAC?

[Validate participants' responses but make sure to cover the following below]:

- *How much alcohol you drink.*
- *The strength of the drink or percent of alcohol (12 oz. beer compared to a Long Island Iced Tea will have a very different percentage of alcohol).*
- *Food eaten along with drinking alcohol will result in a lower, delayed BAC because the alcohol enters the bloodstream at a slower rate.*
- *Type of mixer used. Water mixed with alcohol slows the absorption process, while carbonated beverages will speed it up. Carbon dioxide speeds the alcohol through the stomach and intestine into the bloodstream, creating a rapid rise in BAC.*
- *Tolerance affects how you feel but not the actual content of alcohol in the blood stream (BAC).*
- *Drinking slowly and moderately will increase your chances to maintain your buzz and not dramatically feel the not-so-good effects of alcohol.*

Biphasic Response to Alcohol

So you are at a party... When people start to lose their "buzz," what do they usually do?
Close-ended response expected: DRINK.
Do they get it back?

Close-ended response expected: NO.
What does happen?
Close-ended response expected: they get drunker.

Ask if this buzz is as good as the initial buzz. It's okay to ask students to describe what a buzz is; chances are they are confusing the buzz with being over the limit and being drunk.

Facilitator Dialogue:
Most people are not successful in getting their buzz back after it's gone because of something called the biphasic response of alcohol.

Biphasic refers to the two phases or effects of alcohol on the body.

The first phase consists of feeling stimulated, excited, and euphoric. The other phase consists of depressant effects, such as slowed-down body processes and depressed feelings.

The good feelings are typically associated with the rise in your BAC level. Thus, as you begin consuming alcohol you feel good effects. However, as your BAC rises above .05-.06, you are more likely to experience the not-so-good effects of alcohol.

Draw a graph to illustrate the biphasic effect.

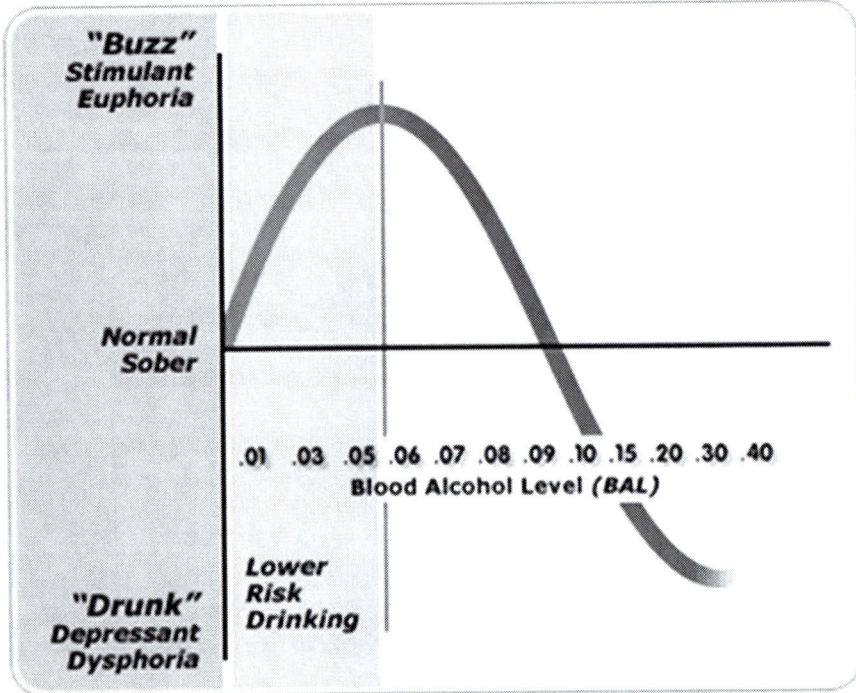

© Hanson, 2007.

The general cultural myth about alcohol is that the more you drink, the more you experience the good effects.

Actually, at a BAC of about .05-.06% most people begin to feel more not-so-good effects of alcohol as compared to the good effects of alcohol. This point is called the point of diminishing returns, meaning that it is difficult to get those good feelings, or buzz, back the way that it felt best. If you drink too much you are more likely to experience the depressant effects of alcohol. This is where the shift occurs and after this point, the body experiences only the depressant effects of alcohol.

Please check your BAC card for your own personal .05-.06 level. It might be helpful to think about how long a party usually lasts, and look at the BAC card for the .05-.06 level and your own personal number of drinks. Once you get to a BAC of .05-.06% you will likely not experience any more intense good feelings.

On the right side of your BAC card is the description of the green, blue, and red zones. If you are going to drink, it is best to stay in your green zone (up to but not exceeding the .05-.06 level). The level of drinking associated with the blue and red zones is linked with increased risk levels.

How many of you know someone who has been hospitalized because of her or his drinking?

What was this experience like for you?

This may happen anywhere around .20 and above.

Symptoms of alcohol poisoning to look out for are hypothermia or cold, clammy skin, slowed breathing (less than 9 breaths per minute), unconsciousness (without being able to be woken up), vomiting while passed out, slow pulse (50 or below and dropping), and no pain response. If you think your friend has alcohol poisoning, call x222 on campus or 911 off campus.

Expectancy Challenges

- *How many of LMU students feel alcohol helps break the ice with people? (LMU—82%)*
- *How many of LMU students feel alcohol enhances social life? (LMU—80%)*
- *How many of LMU students feel alcohol helps facilitate sexual opportunities? (LMU—63%)*

These statistics tell us that many LMU students believe that alcohol has a social expectancy effect. Many people believe in these effects of alcohol, which are called expectancies. They are the beliefs you have about alcohol and they are set for us by our peers, by TV, movies, etc. Research has shown that kids as early as age five have expectancies around alcohol and that these positive expectancies predict heavier drinking and more problems connected to drinking later in life.

Also, many of the reported effects of alcohol are actually expectancy effects. People expect alcohol to make them feel a certain way, so they in fact feel that way. It is the power of mind over physiology, much like the placebo effect.

Many studies have been done to test the placebo effect of alcohol. Half of participants are given alcoholic drinks, while the other half are given non-alcoholic drinks designed to taste and "kick" like real alcoholic drinks. The experimenters give participants some medial performance task to do, such as a puzzle. Some people who were not given alcohol but believed that they were actually showed the same expected impairments in functioning as those who did receive alcohol.

The same has been shown in social situation studies. Half of the participants are given alcohol and half are given a non-alcoholic placebo. People who did not receive any alcohol still show some drunken behavior, especially in awkward or anxious social situations with strangers. Study after study shows many, if not most, of alcohol's purported social effects are really expectancy effects. There is physiological/cross-cultural evidence that alcohol does not account for the observable changes in social behavior that occur when people are drinking. It simply gives them an "excuse" to act in a way that they are capable of acting sober.

Expect

	Alcohol	No Alcohol
Alcohol	Person receives what he or she expects to (alcohol).	Person receives alcoholic beverage when expecting a non-alcoholic one.
No Alcohol/Placebo	Person receives non-alcoholic beverage when expecting alcohol.	Person receives what he or she expects (non-alcoholic beverage).

Receive

The big idea about expectancies is that they are important and they influence how we behave. The purpose of these questions was to help you figure out how you expect alcohol to affect you, and to be aware of these when you drink. Next time you are drinking, think, "What do I expect will result from my drinking?" and think about whether it is actually the alcohol or simply just you (your personality, your social skills) that is allowing these expectations to happen.

Making Motivational Statement/Setting a Behavioral Goal

It is important to set behavioral goals for yourself. I want each of you to make a motivational goal for how you will drink in the next 30 days. This goal can be anything related to your drinking. Write this goal on the sheet provided and fill out the questions that follow. It may be something as simple as, "I will drink less than I do now," or "I will drink only two times per week." Remember, the important message from today's group is to be mindful of your decisions. However you choose to drink is a personal decision. Be aware of how you choose to drink and the reasons why you choose to drink.

Participant Feedback

We are almost finished. The last thing I need you to do is fill out the last sheet in your packet. This is a brief questionnaire assessing this group. When you are finished with that, I will collect it.

Drinking Diary Follow-Up

The last thing we will go over is your diaries. These are logs in which you will keep track of your drinking behavior over the next 12 weeks. At the end of each week, you will be sent a link to an online diary form that you must complete within two days of receiving. It should take no more than 5 minutes to complete. Please make sure you check your email often and complete the diaries the day you receive them.

Be sure to fully explain the diaries and how they are to be completed. Remind them of the sensitive nature of the diary and how it is confidential.

Appendix B
Heads UP Women Intervention Script

This script was devised for a motivational group co-facilitated by two facilitators. The role of each facilitator is indicated by the letter A or letter B for Facilitator A and Facilitator B, respectively, for each of the sections covered in the script. In the sections where both A and B are indicated, both facilitators share responsibility for the section.

A & B – Welcome (5 minutes)
Facilitator Dialogue:
Welcome and thank you for being here for the Heads UP Women Program.
[Facilitators introduce themselves.]
What have you heard about this program?

Briefly, Heads UP is a program with two functions: a long-term research project, which you are all involved in, and alcohol programming events on campus. In general, Heads UP is a program aimed at helping women make the best individual choices about their personal drinking behaviors as well as choices regarding their general health and well-being. We are not an abstinence-based program. Rather, we encourage mindfulness about decisions that affect health and well-being. Our purpose today is to learn more from you about college women and drinking.

A – Review of Informed Consent (5 Minutes)

Please take a look at the form coming around. This is the informed consent form. It states that we will not share your information with anyone. It also provides a description of what will be covered in the group.

Your name will not appear on any forms except the consent form and the sign-in sheet. You will use the sequence number we have provided you on all other forms.

We will keep all of your answers to the questionnaires confidential as well as anything you choose to share with the group today. What questions do you have about the forms or the group?

Please show by a nod of your head that you agree to the informed consent that you completed online.

What you choose to share is up to you. If you choose to share today that would be great and it would be helpful if what will be shared in the room during the groups would stay in the room in order for everyone to feel comfortable. It is important to hear everyone's ideas and opinions, and maintain a mutual respect for one another in our different opinions. For example, we expect that some of you may drink and some of you may not drink and we welcome everyone's opinions in our discussion today.

B – Initial Questionnaire

The initial questionnaire consists of several developed, revised, and validated questionnaires about drinking behavior and drinking-related attitudes and beliefs. Feel free to develop your own questionnaire if you wish to evaluate the effectiveness of your program.

This portion of the program can be completed online if the proper equipment is obtained. Participants can be emailed this questionnaire and asked to fill it out and bring it with them to the group meeting. If surveys are completed online, ask participants if they had any questions regarding the survey. Then continue to the Timeline Followback (TLFB) section. Make sure to review the definition of standard drinks either during the initial question (if completed in the group) or during the TLFB (if the initial questionnaire was completed online).

Facilitator Dialogue:
Can anyone tell me the definition of one standard drink?

One standard drink is considered a 12 oz. beer, a 1.25 oz. shot, a 4 oz. glass of wine, or a mixed drink containing a 1.25 oz. shot of alcohol. Not all mixed drinks contain exactly one shot (or exactly one standard drink). For example, a Long Island Iced Tea has four shots in it and therefore would be considered four standard drinks; the equivalent of four cans of beer. Answer all questions in terms of standard drinks. Are there any questions about standard drinks before we proceed?

Begin completing the initial questionnaire after the informed consent form is signed and passed in. It will take about 15 minutes to complete. Please fill out the questionnaire as accurately and honestly as possible. Remember, all information will be kept confidential and is only being collected for research purposes.

Please read the directions on each page of the questionnaire to ensure accuracy. For questions that ask for a number (for instance the number of days you drank in the last month) indicate only one number, not a range of numbers.

Once you are finished, please pass in your questionnaires.

A – Timeline-Followback Calendaring of Drinking Behavior (10 Minutes)

If it's okay with all of you, we're going to start today with an activity by calendaring the drinking and the non-drinking you've done over the past three months. Together, we are going to come up with how much alcohol you consumed on each day during the past three months. At first this may seem difficult, but if you use a calendar like this one [show the calendar]*, you will be surprised at how well you can remember your drinking days and patterns. A calendar is very useful in helping people recall their drinking.*

Hand out the three-month TLFB calendar with marker dates, holidays, and campus events. Encourage students to complete TLFB independently. Although students will share events together out loud, calendaring of drinking should be done independently. Facilitators might want to consider separating friends or rearranging the seating order so that students are not tempted to work together during the TLFB.

Now let's begin. Let's start with yesterday and go back about three months. Please circle yesterday and go back three months from yesterday and circle that day [announce the date aloud]*. Cross off the days from today on and the days before three months ago.*

As you can see, standard holidays are already marked for you on the calendar to help you recall your activities around these times. What are some other significant dates that have occurred in the past three months? What are some other big on-campus events that you can remember?

Now, come up with any other special events or holidays that have occurred in the past three months that would help your memory. These can be good things that have happened to you or not-so-good things that have happened to you: birthdays, celebrations, hospitalizations, check receipt days, and so on. They can be related to drinking or they can just be other memorable days that have occurred in the past month. We will call these "Marker Days." Fill out your own marker days on your calendars. You can use any marks you want to indicate your marker days; it is irrelevant for us to know what they are. They are simply going to be used to help you remember your drinking and non-drinking.

The idea here is to record the number of drinks you consumed each day. You will go back through each day of the calendar and write the number of standard drinks you consumed on each day. If you had no drinks on a day, mark a zero on the day.

It is important to record your drinking on the calendar in terms of standard drinks. What makes up one standard drink? [Prompt: What do you mean by this?]

One standard drink is equal to one 12 oz. regular beer (a can or a bottle), one 4 oz. glass of wine, one 1.25 oz. shot of hard alcohol (like vodka or whiskey), one mixed drink with one 1.25 oz. shot of hard alcohol, a 10 oz. wine cooler, or an 8 oz. malt liquor.

Facilitators: Show visuals

What kinds of drinks do you normally have? How many standard drinks are included? For example, if you had a 40 oz. bottle of malt liquor, you would indicate that you drank about 5 standard drinks (malt liquor is higher in alcohol content than regular beer). Likewise, if you drank a Long Island Iced Tea with four shots of liquor in it, you would have had four standard drinks. A 12 oz. can of beer would be one standard drink. An "adios" would include about five standard drinks. For instance, you may be holding one glass of a Long Island Iced Tea, but you are actually consuming four standard drinks in that one glass. What questions do you have about standard drinks?

Now, we are going to go back through the calendar every day for the past three months and mark what days you drank and how much you drank. Keep in mind this does not have to be perfect. We want you to be as accurate as possible, but we realize that it is hard for anyone to recall things perfectly. So if you can't recall, for example, whether you drank on a Monday or a Thursday of a certain week, just give it your best guess.

This goes the same for quantity of drinks—just give it your best guess. If you don't remember if you had 20, 21, or 22 drinks, eight, nine, or ten drinks, or two, three, or four drinks for example, just choose the middle of the range; so you would say something like 21 for the first range I mentioned, nine for the second range I mentioned, and three for the final range I mentioned. If you didn't drink at all, mark a zero on that day. What questions do you have?

For now, we are going to start with today and go back through each day of the last two weeks together. You will write the number of drinks you drank on each day that you drank.

Start with today and take the participants back through each day of the calendar for two weeks. Then allow them to fill out the calendar on their own.

We will walk around and help you while filling these out. Remember this doesn't need to be perfect, but please try and be as accurate and honest as possible. Make sure to put down a single number for the amount of drinks, not a range. If you can't remember, just use your best guess.

Then if it makes sense, you can continue to fill out the rest of the three months on your own.

If the participants are having trouble remembering drinking days, prompt them with: What activities do you typically participate in when you drink? Do you drink only on certain nights? Or is there a night when you usually always drink? While watching a television show? On a trip? If they say "a lot," ask them what they mean, and to tell you more.

Facilitator Dialogue:
[When participants are all finished]: *Starting with yesterday we want you to go back over the **past month** and indicate on which drinking days you believe you drank four drinks in a two-hour period. Indicate those days by circling the day. Also, write "M" on the day you drank the most in the past month. If it seems reasonable, we can talk about this later on today.*

If participant questions the four drinks in two-hour period, follow with "if you had four drinks in one setting, generally two to three hours." If there are further questions, instruct participant to use their best guess.

Facilitator Dialogue:
When you are done, please write your participant ID number at the top, flip them over and pass them into one of us. Thank you for filling this out.

A & B – Introductions (5 Minutes)

Facilitator Dialogue:
For judicial participants: Let's now take a moment to introduce ourselves to each other. Please state your first name, your year, where you live, how you ended up here (in Heads UP), and how you feel about being here.

For volunteer participants: Let's now take a moment to introduce ourselves to each other. Please state your first name, where you live, and where you're from. [If you feel that the group is tired or particularly quiet, also ask how they feel].

B – Good and Not-so-good Things about Drinking Discussion (5 Minutes)

We'd like to ask you about the good things and the not-so-good things about drinking. What are the things you enjoy about drinking?

What are the not-so-good things about drinking?

Let participants briefly comment on issues around alcohol that are most salient for them. This section is an introduction to the topic, rather than an exhaustive list and discussion. The following are some examples as generated by previous groups; however, the content of the discussion should be generated by the participants.

Good Things about Drinking: Fun, social, feel more confident, feel more outgoing, gives me something to do, calms me down, it's exciting, it tastes good, it's available, why not?, makes me feel sexy, makes me feel more attractive, helps me bond with people, helps me have honest discussions, helps me cope with things, helps me forget, it's a thrill!

Not-so-good Things about Drinking: Interferes with studying for midterms, increases conflict, isn't compatible with my busy schedule, makes me gain weight, bad for my health, hangovers, spend too much money on alcohol, interferes with my religion, bad things have happened to me when I drank, I lost someone or something important to me, interferes with my grades, I become a different person, I get a bad reputation, I'm not able to meet new people, I can do harm to myself or someone else, people can get mean, I have regrets.

Wrap up with content shared during the discussion—some of the good things were this and some of the not-so-good things were this.

A – Expectancy Challenges (5 Minutes):

The goal of this discussion is to reduce positive drinking expectancies and to increase alternative explanations for enhanced sociability and sexual feelings in situations involving alcohol.

If participants have addressed social issues of drinking during the previous discussion, use their responses here. Otherwise, if not generated by the group, prompt discussion of social expectations of alcohol use. For example, What social effects of alcohol have you noticed?

Facilitator Dialogue:

You have mentioned that alcohol has many social effects linked with it. This is a topic that has interested many researchers and we would like to share some of their work with you. In order to study the effects of alcohol, researchers thought it would be best to create a situation that seemed the most real to college students around drinking. They created a bar lab, where students over 21 could drink and be monitored regarding the effects of alcohol on their behavior. [If possible, show pictures of the bar lab here]. *In these studies, there were four groups. The groups included the various combinations of the following: alcohol v. placebo and expected alcohol v. didn't expect alcohol* [draw graph to illustrate]. *The results were always the same.*

Here it is okay for you to walk up to the PowerPoint chart (or a written chart on a white board) displaying the four conditions and point out the different conditions. Start with the two control conditions (on the diagonal) and then ask what they think happened for the experimental/placebo conditions. Be very clear that the four conditions occurred at different times and not all four at the same time.

Facilitator Dialogue:

For those who expected alcohol, regardless of whether they received alcohol or not, they were more gregarious, outgoing, loud, and social. For those who didn't expect alcohol, regardless of whether they received alcohol or not, they acted less social, less outgoing, and quieter. In fact, those who received alcohol without expecting it attributed the physiological effects, such as feeling warmer and sleepier, to other things in their lives, such as high room temperature and not getting enough rest the night before, respectively. What do you all make of this?

Wrap-up Discussion: Highlight the role of what people expect with regard to their drinking behavior. Share how social and interpersonal things have more to do with expectations and mindset and less to do with alcohol. The physiological effects of the alcohol still occur, but not the social and interpersonal reactions. Ask them about ways to experience the social piece without alcohol. If someone drinks to be funny, for example, it's not actually the alcohol that is helping them but rather their expectation that it will. Maybe ask how they think people felt when they were told they didn't get alcohol.

Thanks. You gave us great input on the good things and the not-so-good things about alcohol use. If it's okay with you, let's talk about alcohol use here at LMU.

B – Normative Data Feedback (10 Minutes)

Facilitator Dialogue:
Let's take a look at what you all think drinking is like here at LMU. I will ask you some questions and I want you to guess what the answers are. The data provided is from the CORE Survey administered to about 1,300 LMU students, with equal representation from each class (about 320 students from each class) in the spring of 2005.

Think of all of the female students at LMU...what percent of all of the female students drink 2 or less days per week?
- *94% of females (6% of female students drank three or more days per week; 8% for women drinkers only).*
- *89% of all LMU students drink 2 or less days per week (11% of all students drink 3 or more days per week).*

What do you think is the average number of drinks consumed per week by LMU female students?
- *2.91 drinks per week for women (for women drinkers only: 3.85 drinks).*
- *4.54 drinks per week for all students.*
- *That means the average person cannot be drinking in excess.*
- *Think about where you fall—Close to the average of your peers? Or outside of the average?*

In the past month, what do you think is the average maximum amount of drinks the typical LMU female student consumed at one time?

- *3.98 drinks at one time for women (for women drinkers only: 5.13 drinks).*
- *5.36 drinks at one time for all students.*
- *Only 49% of women (less than half) drank four or more drinks during their maximum consumption; 51% are having three or fewer drinks during their maximum consumption.*

What does your drinking look like? You might want to think about where you fall in comparison to the averages and what your drinking is like in comparison to your peers here at LMU.

Now if it's cool with you, we are going to talk about how drinking affects sexual experiences here at LMU.

What percentage of the time is alcohol involved in the following experiences here at LMU?
- *forced/unwanted sexual touching (64%)*
- *regretted sexual intercourse (76%)*
- *unwanted sexual intercourse (80%)*

What do you make of all these statistics? What is surprising regarding the statistics? What do these statistics mean to you?

Give feedback for any expressions of surprise from the participants. Present these in groups of three questions and then reflect, unless a "whoa" experience comes up after certain questions. May want to point out for the sexual-experiences questions that with increased consequences, the percent of time alcohol is involved also increases.

A – The Processing of Alcohol (5 minutes)
Alcohol Metabolism

Facilitator Dialogue:
How does alcohol affect men and women differently?

Women become intoxicated after drinking smaller quantities of alcohol than are needed to produce intoxication in men. So even when size is comparable, there are still differences. This is due to three factors:

First, women have lower total body water content than men of comparable size. After alcohol is consumed, it diffuses uniformly into all body water, both inside and outside cells. Women and men are built differently. The average female carries more body fat than the average male (regardless of women's body structure), and thus less water, because body fat contains little water. Consequently, most women have less body water to dilute the alcohol, leaving a higher concentration of alcohol in women's bodies. If you are drinking with a male friend, the same amount of alcohol you drink is being processed more slowly for you than it is for him.

Second, alcohol dehydrogenase is a metabolizing enzyme in the stomach that helps the body get alcohol out of its system. Women have less of this enzyme than men do, so more of what women drink enters the bloodstream as pure alcohol.

Third, women are susceptible to the intoxicating effects of alcohol when their estrogen levels are higher, both premenstrually and when taking birth control pills. There is evidence that women taking birth control pills will absorb alcohol faster causing the intoxicating effects of alcohol to set in with smaller amounts of alcohol. In short, women get drunk more quickly and will stay intoxicated longer.

Women absorb and metabolize alcohol differently than men. What effects that we spoke about have you noticed?

Bring up key point here that match drinking can have different effects for men and women

Alcohol Effects

Facilitator Dialogue:
How does alcohol affect your body physiologically?
Have you heard of some drugs classified as stimulants and other drugs classified as depressants?
Alcohol is interesting because, although it is a depressant drug, it can make people feel "revved up" initially by shutting down different circuits in the brain. When we say the word "depress" we actually mean to slow down. Yet, alcohol is a depressant that initially has stimulating effects.

You can only get to a certain level of feeling good before the depressant effects of alcohol kick in.
Next, if it's okay with you, let's address specific levels of alcohol in your body by addressing your own personal blood alcohol content.

B – Blood Alcohol Content (BAC) Discussion (5 Minutes)

We just mentioned that your body is affected by the amount of alcohol you consume. One way to measure the amount of alcohol in your body is by looking at the amount of alcohol circulating in your blood, or BAC. We are passing around BAC cards and I will explain to you what it means. Please take the card that corresponds with your weight. These cards are specific for women. BAC stands for "Blood Alcohol Content." This is also known as Blood Alcohol Level.

The number represents the concentration of alcohol in your blood. A BAC of .10 means that .1% of your bloodstream is made up of alcohol. Notice these things about your personal cards:

On the top should be your weight and sex. Below are the number of hours spent drinking. On the left side is the number of drinks consumed. Match up the number of drinks consumed with the number of hours spent drinking to find your blood alcohol content. These are represented by the numbers in the middle of the card.

Understanding your BAC could enable you to enjoy the things you like about drinking, drink responsibly, and prevent the not-so-good things about alcohol use from happening.

The cards provided give you an idea of what would happen if you never drank before and consumed a certain amount of alcohol (particularly as referenced in the lower BAC levels). However, you might experience the following at different BAC levels. Please view the levels and corresponding effects on the PowerPoint presentation.

Notice each level and how many drinks it would take for you to get to that level, by looking at your BAC card. Let's highlight a couple of BAC levels.

Go through these levels quickly. If surprise is encountered, reflect after showing the levels.

- *At .02, many people begin to feel relaxed.*
- *At .04, relaxation continues and a buzz develops.*
- *Up to but not exceeding .06, people may have lower inhibitions and sense warmth, feel euphoric, experience intense emotions, and behave in an exaggerated manner. Cognitive judgment is impaired. Up to but not exceeding this point is where you may feel the good things about alcohol.*

- *At .08, motor coordination is impaired, which is why this is the legal driving limit in the state of CA if you are 21 years or over. If you are under 21 years, ANY alcohol use may result in a DUI. Remember that reaction times are slower even with your first drink.*
- *At .10, there is clear deterioration in cognitive judgment and motor coordination. One may experience nausea here.*
- *Between .15-.25 people may experience blackouts.*
- *From .25-.35 people may pass out, lose consciousness, and there is the risk of death.*
- *.40-.45 can be associated with a lethal dose.*

What factors may affect your BAC?

Let participants respond to this question. Correct any false information and provide them with accurate information. Make sure to cover all of the following:

Facilitator Dialogue:
- *First, how much alcohol you drink affects your BAC. If you drink more, you will reach a higher BAC.*
- *Also, the strength of the drink or percent of alcohol (12 oz. beer compared to a Long Island Iced Tea have a very different percentage of alcohol). If you consume 4 oz. of liquor, you will reach a higher BAC than if you consume 4 oz. of wine, or 4 oz. of beer.*
- *Food eaten along with drinking alcohol will result in a delayed BAC because the alcohol enters the bloodstream at a slower rate.*
- *Also, the type of mixer used affects your BAC. Drinking water while consuming alcohol slows the absorption process (or alternating drinks), while carbonated beverages like soda will speed it up. Carbon dioxide speeds the alcohol through the stomach and intestine into the bloodstream, creating a rapid rise in BAC. For instance if you are drinking a rum and coke, you will reach your BAC faster than if you were drinking only rum. The soda acts as a catalyst for the alcohol.*
- *As we mentioned earlier, women reach higher BACs faster and tend to stay intoxicated longer because of the physiological differences between men and women.*
- *Time is the only thing that can reduce your BAC—not coffee, a cold shower, or a run around the block.*

Here you may want to use the "Clone Myself" example. If I were to clone myself and we both have six beers, I would have a higher tolerance than my clone, who is new to drinking. She may be stumbling about and slurring her words, while I stand and talk perfectly, yet our BAC levels would be the same. Why does the clone have an advantage? (The answer is that her body is giving her cues that her BAC is high, making it easier for her to know when to stop, and she doesn't have to spend as much money on alcohol.) Describe conditioning and different settings: how the body overcompensates to prepare for substances and how tolerance is like weight—you can gain or lose it.

A – Biphasic Response of Alcohol (5 minutes)

Facilitator Dialogue:
So you are at a party… When people start to lose their "buzz," what do they usually do?
Close-ended response expected: DRINK.
Do they get it back?
Close-ended response expected: NO.
What does happen?
Close-ended response expected: they get drunker.
Ask if this buzz is as good as the initial buzz. It's okay to ask students to describe what a buzz is—chances are they are confusing the buzz with being over the limit and being drunk.

Facilitator Dialogue:
Most people are not successful in getting their buzz back after it's gone because of something called the biphasic response of alcohol. The general cultural myth about alcohol is that the more you drink, the more you experience the good effects.

Biphasic refers to the two phases or effects of alcohol on the body.

The first phase consists of feeling stimulated, excited, and euphoric. The second phase consists of depressant effects, such as slowed-down body processes and depressed feelings.

The good feelings are typically associated with the rise in your BAC level. Thus, as you begin consuming alcohol you feel good effects. However, as your BAC rises above .05-.06, you are more likely to experience the not-so-good effects of alcohol. This point is called the point of diminishing returns, meaning that it is difficult to get those good feelings or "buzz" back. If you drink too much, you are more likely to experience the depressant effects of alcohol. This is where the shift occurs and after this point, the body experiences only the depressant effects of alcohol.

Draw a graph to illustrate the biphasic effect.

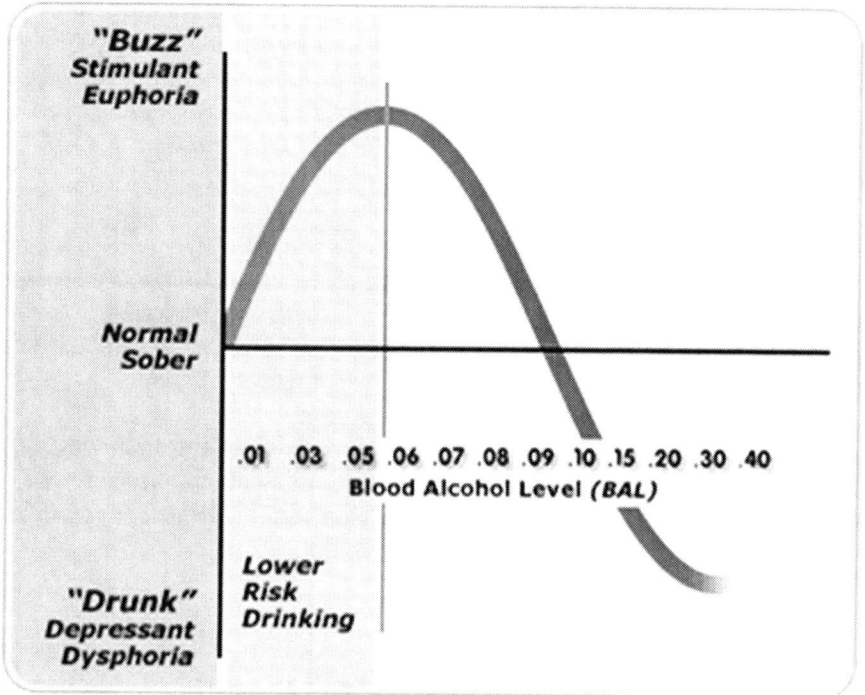

© Hanson, 2007.

Please check your BAC card for your own personal .05-.06 level. It might be helpful to think about how long a party usually lasts, and look at the BAC card for the .05-.06 level and your own personal number of drinks. Once you get to a BAC of .05-.06% you will likely not experience any more intense good feelings.

On the right side of your BAC card is the description of the green, blue, and red zones. If you are going to drink, it is best to stay in your green zone (up to but not exceeding the .05-.06 level). The level of drinking associated with the blue and red zones is linked with increased risk levels.

How many of you know someone who has been hospitalized because of her or his drinking?

What was this experience like for you?

This may happen anywhere around .20 and above.

Symptoms of alcohol poisoning to look out for are hypothermia or cold, clammy skin, slowed breathing (less than 9 breaths per minute), unconsciousness (without being able to be woken up), vomiting while passed out, slow pulse (50 or below and dropping), and no pain response. If you think your friend has alcohol poisoning, call x222 on campus or 911 off campus.

What are some ways you can protect yourself from the riskier consequences (linked to the blue and red zones) from happening to you? What are some strategies that will help prevent the riskier consequences of drinking? Drinking slowly and moderately will increase your chances to maintain your buzz and not dramatically feel the not-so-good effects of alcohol.

Also, include discussion here about protective behaviors and strategies. Examples of protective strategies include: Determine not to exceed a set number of drinks; alternate alcoholic and non-alcoholic drinks; put extra ice in your drink; drink water while drinking alcohol.

A & B – Group Break (5 minutes)

A & B – Return from Break and Questions (5 minutes)

Facilitator Dialogue:
What questions or comments came up for you during the break?

A & B – Reasons for Drinking Discussion (10-15 minutes)

If it's cool with you, let's discuss the reasons women either drink or don't drink and the role alcohol plays in the lives of women. As we discussed before, we are looking to you for information on this topic because you are female college students and can provide us with more specific knowledge about the reasons women at LMU and specifically, all of you, drink alcohol.

Please be as open and honest as you can. Feel free to give your opinions as often as you like. For example, you may feel similarly to what someone else has expressed or you may feel differently, and both of those opinions are important to us.

Use as few closed-ended questions as possible, use a few open-ended questions, and mostly reflect back what participants say in a manner that prompts further discussion of the topic they are describing.

Facilitator Dialogue:
What are the reasons that women drink? What are the reasons women don't drink? What about you specifically?

Information regarding consequences of alcohol use can be assimilated into this discussion. However, the discussion should be generated by the group participants.

Summarize each topic along the way with the overall take home point. End with a double-sided summary/reflection. Make sure that the role of alcohol in relationships is always discussed. If this is not brought up naturally in the group, ask directly "How does alcohol affect your relationships?"

List of topics you may want to address: How does alcohol affect...
- Peer influences/social contexts
- How does drinking impact social situations?
- How is peer pressure a factor in drinking?
- Pre-partying/pre-gaming
- Role of drinking in relationships
- Relationships—how has alcohol affected women's relationships with others?
- Relationships with family
- Friendships
- Romantic relationships
- Sex lives
- Date rape/sexual issues
- Compromising or embarrassing situations
- General health
- Affect-driven drinking
- Tension, mood, boredom
- Studies and/or school performance

B – Decisional Balance (10 Minutes)

Facilitator Dialogue:
Thank you all for being so open and sharing with us your reasons for drinking and not drinking. Next, if it's cool with all of you, we would like you

to record your own personal reasons why you might choose to drink less or maintain your non-drinking behavior.

*Please take a look at this worksheet. For those of you **who consider yourselves drinkers**, up on the top left side of the sheet write **"Not drinking less than I do now"** and go ahead and list your own personal reasons for not drinking less, basically, why you would want to continue drinking, and what your reasons are for drinking. For those of you who **consider yourselves non-drinkers**, please write **"Not staying a non-drinker"** and list your personal reasons why you may want to begin drinking or any obstacles you may run into that may make you think about drinking. You do not have to list 10 reasons, just as many as are personal and relevant for you. You may want to think about what we have discussed today, especially in the discussion we just had.*

Now please go through and rate each reason independently by writing a number between "0" and "10" next to each reason. A "0" rating would be not an important reason to you. A "10" rating would be a highly important reason to you. Keep in mind that you can have more than one item rated at the same number; this is a rating, not a ranking.

*Okay. Now if it makes sense we are going to go on to the next side of the sheet, so on the right side, if **you consider yourself a drinker**, go ahead and write **"Drinking less than I do now"** and list any personal reasons you may have for reducing your drinking. And if **you consider yourself a non-drinker**, go ahead and write **"Staying a non-drinker"** and write your own personal reasons for staying a non-drinker. Why would you not want to begin drinking? Again, you don't have to write 10 reasons, just as many as are important to you.*

Now please go through again and rate each reason on the right side from "0" to "10" just as you did on the left side. Keep in mind that you can have more than one item rated at the same number; this is a rating, not a ranking.

Draw the following ruler for participants to use as a scale.
0---1----2---3----4----5----6----7-----8----9-----10
Not important   Moderately   Extremely

Once you have completed that, give each list an overall rating from "0" to "10," meaning, give each side, all of your reasons on the left together and all of your reasons on the right together, a rating from "0" to "10," indicating how important each side is to you.

We've talked a lot about drinking and drinking less. If you were going to make a change, what would you do? How would you do it?

A – Making Motivational Statement/Setting a Behavioral Goal (5 Minutes)

Now, if it makes sense, we are going to fill out another sheet. The first question asks you about your readiness to change your drinking; if you've ever thought about it or if you have changed your behavior already. Please circle the number that corresponds to where you are currently in terms of your change.

Next, we would like to set a personal, behavioral goal. What could you do if you wanted to drink less? Please think of a motivational goal for how you will drink in the next 30 days. It may be something as simple as, "I will drink less than I do now" or "I will drink only two times per week" or "I will continue to not drink." This goal can be anything related to your drinking. Write your goal down on the form and the card provided. The card is for you to keep.

Please complete the rest of the sheet. When you are done, please write your ID number on top, turn them over, and pass them in.

Remember, the important message from today's group is to be mindful of your decisions. However you choose to drink is a personal decision. Be aware of how you choose to drink and the reasons why you choose to drink.

Now let's share our behavioral goals. What are some barriers that we may experience in attempting to achieve these goals? What are your strategies for handling these challenges and difficulties?

B – Drinking Diary Follow-Up (5 Minutes)

Here we explain how diaries will be completed for the next 10 weeks (if volunteer participant) or the next 12 weeks (if judicial participant). Depending on what your institution decides, diary completion may differ. Below is one example.

Facilitator Dialogue:
Now you have completed the first part of the project, and I am going to explain the second part. For the next 10 weeks (12 for judicial participants),

you will receive an email from us to your email account. The email will contain a link to a survey, and it will be set up the same way as the initial survey. Just click on the link to complete the survey. The survey is very short, only about 5-10 minutes, and asks you how many drinks you had on each of the days of the week as well as a few health-related questions. Please complete the diary as soon as you receive it. Since today is _____, you will receive the first email next _____. Watch for the email every _____. Please be sure to contact us immediately if you do not receive the email or if the link does not work. Also, we want to reiterate to you that everything that you complete, here or online, is completely confidential and is never associated with any identifying information.

A & B – Participant Feedback (5 Minutes)

Finally, we'd like to ask you to please complete the Participant Feedback sheet, which asks you what was helpful and not helpful about the session. This information is very helpful for us in improving the project in the future.

We have compiled a brochure about the consequences of alcohol as well as references to additional information, should you be interested in learning more about these topics. Once you are finished, please come up to one of us, and we will give you your brochure and your check.

We thank you for your participation!

137

References

Allen, J. P., Litten, R. Z., Fertig, J. B., & Babor, T. (1997). A review of research on the Alcohol Use Disorders Identification Test (AUDIT). *Alcoholism: Clinical and Experimental Research, 21,* 613-619.

Anderson, D. S., & Gadaleto, A. (2001). *Results of the 2000 College Alcohol Survey: Comparison with 1997 Results and Baseline Year.* Center for the Advancement of Public Health, George Mason University, Fairfax, VA.

Babor, T. F., & Grant, M. (1989). From clinical research to secondary prevention: International collaboration in the development of the Alcohol Use Disorders Identification Test (AUDIT). *Alcohol Health and Research World, 13,* 371-374.

Bachman, J. G., & Johnston, L. D. (1978). *The Monitoring the Future project: Design and procedures.* (Monitoring the Future Occasional Paper no. 1.) Ann Arbor, MI: Institute for Social Research. 67 pp.

Baer, J. S., Kivlahan, D. R., Blume, A. W., McKnight, P., & Marlatt, G. A. (2001). Brief intervention for heavy-drinking college students: 4-year follow-up and natural history. *American Journal of Public Health, 91,* 1310-1316.

Barnett, N. P., Tevyaw, T. O., & Fromme, K. (2004). Brief alcohol interventions with mandated or adjudicated college students. *Alcoholism: Clinical & Experimental Research, 28*(6), 966-975.

Brown, J. M., & Miller, W. R. (1993). Impact of motivational interviewing on participation and outcome in residential alcoholism treatment. *Psychology of Addictive Behaviors, 7*(4), 211-218.

Burke, B. L., Arkowitz, H., & Menchola, M. (2003). The efficacy of motivational interviewing: A meta-analysis of controlled clinical trials. *Journal of Consulting & Clinical Psychology, 71*(5), 843-861.

Higher Education Research Institute. Cooperative Institutional Research Program (CIRP), CIRP Institutional Profile, 2005.

Clapp, J., & McDonnell, A. L. (2000). The relationship of perceptions of alcohol promotion and peer drinking norms to alcohol problems reported by college students. *Journal of College Student Development, 41,* 19-26.

Presley, C. A., Meilman, P. W., & Lyerla, R. (1994). Development of the Core Alcohol and Drug Survey: Initial findings and future directions. *Journal of American College Health, 42,* 248-255.

CORE Institute. CORE Alcohol and Drug Survey. Southern Illinois University, Carbondale: Author, 2005.

DeJong, W. (1998). What college presidents can do about student drinking. *About Campus (July–August),* 12-17.

DeJong, W., & Linkenbach, J. (1999). Telling it like it is: Using social norms marketing campaigns to reduce student drinking. *American Association for Higher Education Bulletin, 32,* 11-16.

Dunn, C., Deroo, L., & Rivara, F. P. (2001). The use of brief interventions adapted from motivational interviewing across behavioral domains: A systematic review. *Addiction, 96*(12), 1725-1742.

Engs, R. C., Diebold, B. A., & Hanson, D. J. (1996). The drinking patterns and problems of a national sample of college students, 1994. *Journal of Alcohol and Drug Education, 41,* 13-33.

Engs, R. C., & Hanson, D. J. (1985). The drinking patterns and problems of college students: 1983. *Journal of Alcohol and Drug Education, 31*(1), 65-83.

Foote, J., DeLuca, A., Magura, S., Warner, A., Grand, A., Rosenblum, A., & Stahl, S. (1999). A group motivational treatment for chemical dependency. *Journal of Substance Abuse Treatment, 17* (3), 181-192.

Frezza, M., DiPadova, C., Pozzato, G., Terpin, M., Baraona, E., & Lieber, C. S. (1990). High blood alcohol levels in women: The role of decreased gastric alcohol dehydrogenase and first-pass metabolism. *New England Journal of Medicine, 322*(2), 95-99.

Gladwell, M. (2000). *The Tipping Point: How Little Things Can Make a Big Difference.* New York: Little, Brown and Company.

Gleason, N. A. (1994). Preventing alcohol abuse by college women: A relational perspective 2. *Journal of American College Health, 43*(1), 15-25.

Greenbaum, T. L. (1993). *The handbook for focus group research (rev. and exp. ed.).* New York: Lexington Books/Macmillan, Inc.

Haines, M., & Spear, S. F. (1996). Changing the perception of the norm: A strategy to decrease binge drinking among college students. *Journal of American College Health, 45,* 134-140.

Hanson, D. J. (1997-2007). How alcohol affects us: The biphasic curve. *Alcohol Problems and Solutions.* Retrieved December 2, 2008, from http://www2.potsdam.edu/hansondj/healthissues/1100827422.html

Henry, S., Lange, J. E., & Wilson, L. (2004, October 16-19). *Evaluation of e-CHUG integrated into two classroom-based alcohol interventions.* Poster presented at the U.S. Department of Education's 18th Annual National Meeting on Alcohol, Other Drug Abuse and Violence Prevention in Higher Education, Washington, DC.

Hingson, R., Hereen, T., Winter, M. R., & Wechsler, H. (2005). Magnitude of alcohol-related mortality and morbidity among U.S. college students ages 18-24: Changes from 1998 to 2001. *Annual Review of Public Health, 26,* 259-279.

Johnston, L. D., O'Malley, P. M., & Bachman, J. G. (2000). Monitoring the Future national survey results on drug use, 1975-1999, Volume II: College students and adults age 19-40 (NIH Publication no. 00-4803). Rockville, MD: National Institute on Drug Abuse.

Jones, B. M., & Jones, M. K. (1976). Women and alcohol: Intoxication, metabolism and the menstrual cycle. In Greenblatt, M., and Schuckit, M. A., eds. *Alcoholism problems in women and children.* New York: Grune & Stratton, 103-136.

LaBrie, J., & Earleywine, M. E. (2000). Sexual risk behaviors and alcohol: Higher base rates revealed using the unmatched-count technique. *Journal of Sex Research, 37,* 321-326.

LaBrie, J. W. (2002). Weighing the pros and cons: A brief motivational intervention reduces risk associated with drinking and unsafe sex. *Unpublished doctoral dissertation*, University of Southern California.

LaBrie, J. W., Lamb, T., Pedersen, E. R., & Quinlan, T. (2006). A group Motivational Interviewing intervention reduces drinking and alcohol-related consequences in adjudicated college students. *Journal of College Student Development, 47*(3), 267-280.

LaBrie, J. W., Pedersen, E. R., & Buckley, K. (2006, in review). Reducing alcohol risk in adjudicated college students: Further validation of a group motivational enhancement intervention. *Journal of College Student Development.*

LaBrie, J. W., Pedersen, E. R., Earleywine, M., & Olsen, H. (2006). Reducing heavy drinking in college males with the decisional balance: Analyzing an element of motivational interviewing. *Addictive Behaviors, 31,* 254-263.

LaBrie, J. W., Pedersen, E., Lamb, T., & Bove, E. (2006). Heads UP! A nested intervention with freshmen male college students to promote responsible drinking. *Journal of American College Health, 54,* 301-304.

LaBrie, J. W., Pedersen, E. R., Lamb, T., & Quinlan, T. (2007). A campus-based group motivational intervention reduces problematic drinking in freshmen male college students. *Addictive Behaviors, 32,* 889-901.

LaBrie, J. W., Quinlan, T., Schiffman, J., & Earleywine, M. (2005). Performance of alcohol and safer sex rulers compared to readiness to change questionnaires. *Psychology of Addictive Behaviors 19*(1), 112-115.

LaBrie, J. W., Tawalbeh, S., Huchting, K., Pedersen, E. R., Thompson, A., Neighbors, C., Shelesky, K., & Larimer, M. (2008). A randomized motivational enhancement prevention group reduces alcohol risk in first year college women. *Psychology of Addictive Behaviors, 22*(1), 149-155.

Larimer, M. E. & Cronce, J. M. (2002). Identification, prevention, and treatment: A review of individual-focused strategies to reduce problematic alcohol consumption by college students. *Journal of Studies on Alcohol, Supp. 14,* 148-163.

Lincourt, P., Kuettel, T. J., & Bombardier, C. H. (2002). Motivational interviewing in a group setting with mandated clients: A pilot study. *Addictive Behaviors, 27*(3), 381-391.

Lo, C. C. (1995). Gender differences in collegiate alcohol use. *Journal of Drug Issues, 25*(4), 817-837.

Mara, J. R. (2000). *The view from the president's office: The leadership of change.* Paper prepared for the Panel on Prevention and Treatment of College Alcohol Problems, National Advisory Council on Alcohol Abuse and Alcoholism, National Institute on Alcohol Abuse and Alcoholism.

McCaul, M. E., & Furst, J. (1994). Alcoholism treatment in the United States. *Alcohol Health & Research World, 18,* 253-260.

Miller, W. R., & Rollnick, S. (1991). *Motivational interviewing: Preparing people to change addictive behavior.* New York: Guilford Press.

Miller, W. R., & Rollnick, S. (2002). *Motivational interviewing: Preparing people to change* (2nd Ed.). New York: Guilford Press.

National Institute on Alcohol Abuse and Alcoholism. (1999). Are women more vulnerable to alcohol effects? Alcohol Alert No. 46. Rockville, MD: U.S. Department of Health and Human Services.

National Institute on Alcohol Abuse and Alcoholism. (2001). Alcoholism: Getting the facts. Retrieved on 3/14/05 from http://www.niaaa.nih.gov/publications/booklet.htm.

National Institute on Alcohol Abuse and Alcoholism (NIAAA). (2002). *A call to action: Changing the culture of drinking at U.S. colleges.* NIH Pub. No. 02-5010. Bethesda, MD: NIAAA.

Noonan W. C., & Moyers, T. B. (1997). Motivational interviewing: A review. *Journal of Substance Abuse 2,* 8-16.

O'Malley, P. M., & Johnston, L. D. (2002). Epidemiology of alcohol and other drug use among American college students. *Journal of Studies on Alcohol, 14,* 23-39.

Perkins, H. W. (2000). Research on women's drinking patterns: Q&A with Wes Perkins. *Catalyst, 6*(1), 6-7.

Perkins, H. W. (2002). Social norms and the prevention of alcohol misuse in collegiate contexts. *Journal of Studies on Alcohol Supplement, 14,* 164-172.

Perkins, H. W., & Wechsler, H. (1996). Variation in perceived college drinking norms and its impact on alcohol abuse: A nationwide study. *Journal of Drug Issues, 26,* 961-974.

Prochaska, J. O., & DiClemente, C. C. (1984). *The transtheoretical approach: Crossing traditional boundaries of treatment.* Homewood, IL: Dow Jones-Irwin.

Rollnick, S., Heather, N., & Bell, A. (1992). Negotiating behavioural change in medical settings: The development of brief motivational interviewing. *Journal of Mental Health (UK), 1*(1), 25-37.

Rollnick, S., Heather, N., Gold, R., & Hall, W. (1992). Development of a short 'readiness to change' questionnaire for use in brief opportunistic intervention among excessive drinkers. *British Journal of Addiction, 87,* 743-754.

Rollnick, S., & Miller, W. R. (1995). What is motivational interviewing? *Behavioural & Cognitive Psychotherapy, 23*(4), 325-334.

Rosenhow, D. J. (1998). Alcoholism. In Blechman, E. A., & Brownell, K. D. (Eds.), *Behavioral medicine and women: A comprehensive handbook.* New York: Guilford Press, 402-406.

San Diego State University Research Foundation. Electronic Check Up To Go (e-Chug). Copyright 2006.

Steiner, J. W., Woodall, W. G., & Yeagley, J. A. (2005). The e-Chug: A randomized, controlled study of a web-based binge drinking intervention with college freshmen. Poster presentation, Society for Prevention Research.

Stewart, D. W., & Shamdasani, P. N. (1990). *Focus groups: Theory and practice.* London: Sage.

Stone, G. L., & Lucas, J. (1994). Disciplinary counseling in higher education: A neglected challenge. *Journal of Counseling & Development, 72*(3), 234-238.

Van Sickle, D., & Sokolow, B. A. (2006). Web-based approaches to alcohol and other drug interventions. *Campus Safety and Student Development, 7,* 49-64.

Vince-Whitman, C., & Cretella, M. (1999). Alcohol use by college women: Pattern, reasons, results, and prevention. *Catalyst, 5*(2), 4-5.

Walters, S. T., Gruenewald, D. A., Miller, J. H., & Bennett, M. E. (2001). Early findings from a disciplinary program to reduce problem drinking by college students. *Journal of Substance Abuse, 20,* 89-91.

Walters, S. T., Matson, S. A., & Harris, T. R. (2005). *A controlled trial of web-based feedback for college freshman.* University of Texas School of Public Health, Dallas Regional Campus, Dallas, TX 75390.

Wechsler, H., Davenport, A., Dowdall, G., Moeykens, B., & Castillo, S. (1994). Health and behavioral consequences of binge drinking in college: A national survey of students at 140 campuses. *Journal of the American Medical Association, 272,* 1672-1677.

Wechsler, H., Lee, J. E., Kuo, M., & Lee, H. (2000). College binge drinking in the 1990's: A continuing Problem: Results of the Harvard School of Public Health 1999 College Alcohol Study. *Journal of American College Health , 48,* 1999-210.

Wechsler, H., Lee, J. E., Kuo, M., Seibring, M., Nelson, T. F., & Lee, H. (2002). Trends in college binge drinking during a period of increased prevention efforts: Findings for 4 Harvard School of Public Health College Alcohol Study surveys, 1993-2001. *Journal of American College Health, 50*(5), 203-217.

Wechsler, H., Moeykens, B., & Davenport, A. (1995). The adverse impact of heavy episodic drinkers on other college students. *Journal of Studies on* Alcohol, *56*(6), 628-634.

Wechsler, H., Molnar, B. E., & Davenport, A. E. (1999). College alcohol use: A full or empty glass? *Journal of American College Health, 47*(6), 247-252.

Wechsler, H., & Nelson, T. F. (2001). Binge drinking and the American college student: What's five drinks? *Psychology of Addictive Behaviors, 15*(4), 287-291.

Wilson, L., Henry, S., & Lange, J. (2005). *Evaluation of e-Chug integrated into two classroom interventions.* Presented at the 4th Annual CSU Alcohol Education Conference, San Jose, CA.

World Health Organization (WHO). (2005). About WHO. Retrieved 3/14/05 from http://www.who.int/about/en/.

Young, A. M., Morales, M., McCabe, S. E., Boyd, C. J., & D'Arcy, H. (2005). Drinking like a guy: Frequent binge drinking among undergraduate women. *Substance Use & Misuse, 40,* 241-267.

Glossary

Blood Alcohol Content (BAC) - the amount of alcohol in your blood, or percent concentration of alcohol in your blood. This can be calculated using one's sex (female/male), weight, and number of standard drinks consumed each hour.

Binge Drinking - 4 or more standard drinks in a 2-hour period or less for women and 5 or more standard drinks in a 2-hour period or less for men (Wechsler et al., 2002).

The following definitions were used in Heads UP Men research project and were conceived by Wechsler et al. 2002:

Frequent Binge Drinker - A person who binge drank 3 or more times for the 2 weeks prior to the intervention.

Binge Drinker - A person who binge drank less than 3 times in the 2 weeks prior to the intervention.

Non-Binge Drinker - A person who consumed alcohol in the 2 weeks prior to the intervention, however, did not binge drink.

Non-Drinker - A person who didn't drink at all one month prior to the intervention.

Cooperative Institutional Research Program (CIRP) - "a national longitudinal study of the American higher education system" (http://www.gseis.ucla.edu/heri/cirp.html, Retrieved on 3/11/05).

Cognitive-Behavioral Skills-Based Programs - Alcohol prevention and intervention programs that focus on the impact of cognitions on drinking behavior. These programs often include other than cognitive components. For example, skills training components, both alcohol-specific and general life skills (e.g., stress management) may be included (Larimer & Cronce, 2002).

CORE - The Core Institute develops and produces drug and alcohol assessment and research. The Core Institute developed the Core Alcohol and Drug Survey, which was used in the Heads UP Men Program and is used on colleges nationwide. The Core Alcohol and Drug Survey provides much of the normative data that is shared with participants in the Heads UP Men intervention.

Electronic Check-Up to Go (e-CHUG) - A brief assessment and feedback tool that can be administered online. The e-CHUG is an electronic form of the paper-and-pencil assessment tool, the Check-Up to Go (CHUG). This tool provides normative feedback as well as feedback about personal risk factors for drinking (Walters, Van Sickle, & Moyer).

Education/Awareness Intervention Programs - Alcohol prevention and intervention programs that provide information regarding the negative consequences, including health risks, of alcohol consumption. In addition to providing information, education and/or awareness intervention, programs may also focus on clarifying values of participants, groups, and the university at large. Finally, these programs may include a normative reeducation component whereby participants are provided with campus norms regarding drinking by their peers (Larimer & Cronce, 2002).

Emotion-Focused Coping Skills - Skills that enable a person to handle a stressor by regulating the emotions associated with the stressor (Folkman & Lazarus,1980).

Expectancy Challenges - A component of the Heads UP Men intervention that asks participants to consider the expected effects of alcohol on them and provides information to participants about the actual effects of alcohol on the body. Further, the role of expectations in creating situations, including anticipating the effects of alcohol, was addressed in the Heads UP Men intervention.

Motivational/Feedback-Based Programs - Alcohol prevention and intervention programs focused on increasing motivation to alter drinking behavior though individual or group motivational techniques, skills-training, and individualized feedback.

Nested Model - Type of intervention employed in the Heads UP Men program whereby the expected results of the group intervention are also expected to impact the participants' larger contexts, including the student body at large and the community.

National Institute on Alcohol Abuse and Alcoholism (NIAAA) - Federal entity created to help address the public health problems of alcohol abuse and alcoholism through research and alcohol-related work.

Normative Reeducation - Alcohol intervention programs that aim to alter drinking behavior by highlighting the discrepancy between actual and perceived norms of drinking behavior. Peers typically present the normative data in these programs (Larimer & Cronce, 2002).

Prevention and Intervention Strategies - Community and public health interventions based on levels of concern and risk.

Primary Prevention Strategy - Prevention strategies designed to maintain health or intervene with low-risk groups, for example, by providing alcohol education to children.

Secondary Prevention Strategy - Programs that target high-risk individuals and groups in an effort to prevent a particular health or community concern, for example, by providing information to children of alcoholics.

Tertiary Intervention Strategy - Programs that intervene with individuals or groups with specific health or community concerns or problems, for example, by using motivational interviewing techniques with individuals who have had problems because of their alcohol use.

Problem-focused Coping Skills - Skills that enable a person to handle a stressor by actively addressing the problem that is creating the stressor (Folkman & Lazarus, 1980).

Relapse Prevention Model (Marlatt & Gordon, 1985) - A cognitive-behavioral method of evaluating risk as well as strategies to prevent relapse in alcohol use. Methods utilized in relapse prevention include identification and understanding high-risk conditions and increasing ability to cope with vulnerability to relapse (Larimer, Palmer, & Marlatt, 1999).

Standard Drink - One standard drink is considered a 12 oz. beer, a 1.5 oz. shot, a 4 oz. glass of wine, or a mixed drink containing a 1.5 oz. shot of alcohol (NIAAA, 2001).

Values Clarification - Alcohol intervention programs aimed at helping participants identify their overall values. Through the process of values clarification, participants may realize their alcohol use might interfere with maintaining values and achieving goals (Sine, 1976).

World Health Organization (WHO) - The United Nations' health organization promoting overall health in the world, including the physical, mental, and social health of all people (WHO, 2005).